A Reader of Curious Books

Arthur Machen

Darkly Bright Press

Catalog Number 010

ISBN: 979-8-9863904-8-2

darkly bright
press · design

www.darklybrightpress.com

A READER OF CURIOUS BOOKS.

For the Curious Reader

A strange breed is the bibliophile. For said sufferer—that being defined as an adorer of books, and that being further defined as a true and concrete incarnation—nothing is more satisfying than gently cradling a faded spine whilst opening the musty, dry leaves of a cherished or forgotten tome from another age of man. The poetry of verso and recto intones a sacred song, the threading of the binding acts as sinew tying flesh to bone, the dark gloss of imprinted letters forming a secret language in an ancient font... this is the lonely rhapsody of the bibliophile.

But do not be misled. This is not gross materialism. Rather it is acknowledgment of the physical reality by which an ineffable joy is expressed. The antiquarian book is not a dry, dead thing, but it is a living relic. It is a symbol, a hieroglyph if you will, that points to truths more real than the Linotype of its pages.

One man who never suffered from this sort of mad devotion was Arthur Machen. He did not care one jot about first or limited editions. In fact, he bore a surprising indifference to the historical issues of his own books. More than once, he wrote on the maladjusted temperament of book collectors, yet it always seemed to be a mild bit of scolding. Perhaps I am wrong, but I carry the belief that while Machen did not imbibe in the habit, he still felt some sympathy for this misfortunate race of man. He wrote as much in one of the insightful essays which comprises *Dog and Duck*, though the focus in this instance centered on gambling. Again, he did not bet on the horses, but believed the unsaid and misunderstood desire of all gamblers is centered in their search for mystery and wonder.

Folly perhaps, but are we not also on the track of so lofty a goal?

This curious book that you hold in your hands is an attempt to track down mystery by bringing to print essays and articles, which have remained unread and forgotten for nearly a century and a half. Each is a small revelation, a brief glimpse into obscurity. Perhaps most would pass over such bits of bone with indifference, but there are those of us who know better.

Hopefully, the author of these fragments will look kindly upon our affliction from his happy place.

Arthur Machen in the 1880s

Inauspiciously, Machen's long literary career began at the age of seventeen with the self-publication of a thin pamphlet entitled *Eleusinia* (1881) which is comprised of a single poem. However, its author grew discontent with its existence in later years. Reportedly, he destroyed a number of copies and inadvertently created a martyr in the form of a highly desired and exceedingly rare collector's item. Soon after its lackluster debut, Machen abandoned poetry for prose.

As the first half of the decade continued, Machen spent periods in the wilderness of London punctuated by respites at his childhood home in Wales. While living in the former, the young man suffered great poverty and loneliness which is excellently recounted in his memoirs published during the 1920s. After failing an exam to enter the Royal College of Surgeons, Machen turned to a variety of occupations including tutoring. Amidst the disappointments of daily privation, Machen sought refuge by wandering the city and writing in his hovel of a room. An extant product of this experience is *The Anatomy of Tobacco*, a truly strange but enticing book that is part paean to smoking and part pastiche on scholastic logic.

Through a strange set of circumstances, Machen was referred to publisher George Redway (1859-1934) who agreed to publish the book albeit with financial support from the writer. It appeared in bookstores in 1884. The relationship continued with paid work after Redway commissioned the young writer to translate *The Heptameron* into English. During the same period, Redway offered him a regular salary of £60 per annum to catalogue books for advertisements. Among his assignments, Machen compiled a large cache of occult material for Redway's catalogues.

However, Machen's tenure with Redway was interrupted in 1885 by the death of his mother for which he traveled back to Wales. While there, he began his second book, *The Chronicles of Clemendy*, a romantic and chivalric saga centered in a glorious Gwent which would find release in 1888. Returning to London, he resumed employment under Redway. While much of the cataloging work may have felt mundane, Machen was allowed some creative freedom when preparing an advertising pamphlet purporting to be a chapter from *Don Quijote de la Mancha*. It replicated the library sequence from the classic novel, a subject which will reappear in the pages of this volume.

The year 1887 would prove pivotal for the aspiring writer. In his classic study, Sweetser writes, "...Redway made him editor of *Walford's Antiquarian*, for which he also wrote many unsigned filler articles." While this is certainly true, Redway retained editorship of the magazine while entrusting his young employee with much of the workload. In this capacity, Machen reviewed and produced pieces for books on a wide range of competencies and fields. Also, it is likely that he created much of the fodder comprising the monthly sections of "Collectanea" and "News and Notes," by writing shorter material, selecting the contributions of other writers and choosing curious excerpts from older sources to satisfy the space requirements.

However, steady and demanding work aside, the year provided other significant changes. During this period, Machen met a man who would provide lifelong friendship, the author and mystic Arthur Edward Waite (1857-1942). Waite would grant comfort and support in dark days ahead while providing publishing opportunities for Machen, a reciprocal arrangement which began by allowing space for Waite in the pages of *Walford's*. In late August, Machen married his first wife Amelia Hogg (1850-1899). Less than a month later, Machen's father died leaving him a small inheritance. This last development allowed him some financial stability after the closing of the magazine in November. By that time, Machen had gained enough confidence and experience to pursue the path of being a professional writer, and it would be in the decade of the 90s that Machen would produce some of his best and most enduring work.

A Lost Bookshelf

This volume reprints for the first time, a collection of material penned by Machen for the *Walford's Antiquarian* magazine. It includes all the previously identified essays and book reviews and a choice selection of material written or edited by Machen for the Collectanea and News and Notes sections of the magazine. Almost without exception, Machen's contributions went unsigned. While we occasionally find a piece attributed to his curious pen-name of Leolinus, only twice does the name of Arthur Machen appear in the pages of the magazine: first, in an advertisement for his translation of *The Heptameron*, and second, as the writer of an essay on heraldry. The basis for inclusion comes from the indispensable work performed by Adrian Goldstone and Wesley D. Sweetser in *A Bibliography of Arthur Machen* (1965).

For the Machen enthusiast, or the causal reader of literary lives, this material presents an image of the writer at a critical juncture. Pragmatically speaking, Machen is learning to write by the act of doing so. Here, we find the earliest collection of his nonfiction work which would later lead to hundreds of journalistic articles, magazine submissions on varied topics and essays on literary and religious criticism. A writer develops his craft by hard work, and here, we find a workshop.

Furthermore, the work displayed in *A Reader of Curious Books* paints an intellectual portrait of Machen as a young man. All of the writer's future themes and favorite subjects can be found in its pages: Christian history and liturgy, folklore, early man, the history of world literature, psychic phenomenon, orthodoxy versus heresy—to name only a few. From the material reviewed, one may find topics for future narratives, incidents for novels and even a phrase which will become the title for a short story. However, already well-read, Machen is not merely reading and writing on these subjects, but he can be seen holding his own with the material. Truly, he may have felt somewhat out of depth in certain areas, such as the Bank of England, but for the most part he is articulate and knowledgeable, and there is a sense that he adds to the conversation.

But there is another opportunity for growth. The dispute with Poe expert John Henry Ingram can be seen as a moment of stone tumbling for Machen. Once polished, his skills for polemics and debating will be showcased in future essays for *The Academy* and other publications.

For the certified bibliophile, a lover of literary exploration or the merely curious, a collection of this sort justifies itself. The archaic dispatches are both entertaining for the quality of the prose and interesting for the array of arcane subjects covered. For the modern reader, the forgotten books become living characters with each title owing its existence to the simple suggestion that it does exist. An obtuse debate upon the effect of ancient geographers upon the mind of Roderick Usher only adds to the obscure proceedings. Certainly, it would be possible for a dedicated enthusiast to hunt down each of these tomes, but the mystery would then be dispelled. In a sense, this lost bookshelf functions best as does the library of Don Quijote—a dusty chamber of the possibly dangerous, perhaps banal books which feed the imagination of man... that mad mammal.

Christopher Tompkins

A Reader of Curious Books

Arthur Machen

Darkly Bright Press

Editor's Note

From the outset of his tenure at the magazine, Machen managed to stir a small measure of controversy after penning the following opinion piece. The conversation it spurred ensued over the course of four issues, but is collected together here for ease of use. Before it begins, an explanation in the form of a brief *dramatis personæ* may be useful.

Leolinus. Machen signed the piece and his subsequent response under this strange pen name which was a favorite alias for the writer during the 1880s. It first appears as the "author" of *The Anatomy of Tobacco* (1884) in its complete and whimsical form of "Leolinus Siluriensis, Professor of Fumifical Philosophy in the University of Brentford." The book is an odd concoction, part devotion to smoking, part satire on the academic essay. "Siluriensis" is a reference to the Silures, an ancient tribe of South-West Wales, Machen's homeland. Like Leolinus, it will appear in other places in Machen's bibliography. After his work at *Walford's Antiquarian*, he employs Leolinus for the name for the "scribe" in *The Chronicles of Clemendy* (1888), a series of romantic adventures narrated in archaic diction. Both books reflect his association with George Redway. The *nom de plume* will surface again in the pages of this volume, but the majority of Machen's numerous contribution went unattributed. Only once did he sign his true name to an article.

John Henry Ingram. Machen's feisty opponent is best remembered for his dedicated defense of Poe's legacy in response to Rufus Wilmot Griswold's work, often considered a character assassination of the legendary writer. As this exchange illustrates, and as Machen clearly states, Ingram took his self-appointed mission seriously. He is credited with producing a well-researched and reliable biography of his celebrated idol.

No doubt, Leolinus's observation pricked a nerve with Ingram, but despite the latter's assumption, Machen meant no injury to Poe, a writer he also respected and wrote about on many occasions. Interestingly, one of his best tales *N* (1936), speaks of a Poe enthusiast's strange visit to Stoke Newington, a section of London boasting both the site of a school Poe once attended as well as the residence of Mr. Ingram.

A READER OF CURIOUS BOOKS.

Vol. XI, January 1887, p.68

Sir,—In one of Edgar Poe's "Tales of Mystery"—I believe the "Fall of the House of Ussher *[sic]*"—we have some passages in the life of a singularly morbid gentleman who was addicted to reading of a singularly morbid type. A list, however, is given of his favourite works, and from what I know of some of these I should be inclined to think the poor gentleman would be bored rather than awed or mystified. One of these books is Campanella's "City of the Sun,"[1] which is an account of an "Ideal Commonwealth" of the Socliastic *[sic]* kind, not in the least mysterious or awe-inspiring. In fact, Poe made the same mistake about Campanella's "Civitas Solis" that Mr. Gosse[2] is said to have made about Harrington's "Ocean."[3] Another volume to which the hero of this weird tale was vastly addicted was "Pomponius Mela,"[4] wherein (we are told) he delighted himself with the description of Ægipans and their mystic dances. But in Mela's work "De Situ Orbis" there is but the merest mention of Ægipans, in the fourth and eighth chapters:—"Intra (si credere libet) vix jam homines, magisque semiferi, Ægipanes, et Blemmyæ, et Gamphasantes, et Satyri sine tectis passim ac sedibus vagi habent potius terras quam habitant." In Solinus,[5] indeed, there is a much fuller account; but, for a person with a taste for occult literature, the ancient geographers would prove but dull reading.

LEOLINUS

---

1 Tommaso Campanella (1568-1639), a Dominican friar, composed *Civitas Solis* (1602) while imprisoned during the Inquisition. The book describes a utopian theocratic state in which all property, including women and children, are held in common. The occult interest in City of Sun, and thereby Poe's purpose for his character Usher, may

A READER OF CURIOUS BOOKS.

Vol. XI, February 1887, p.137-138

Sir,—In your last number, under the above title, an attack was made upon Edgar Poe's literary knowledge. Your correspondent's letter is one series of misstatements. Poe's tale, which is not correctly titled by "Leolinus," does not contain a word about the "mystic dances" of the Ægipans, any more than Mr. Gosse ever mentioned Harrington's "Ocean." As regards the character of Campanella's and Pomponius Mela's works, your correspondent's opinion is quite opposite to that of the readers of both past and present centuries, including—

JOHN HENRY INGRAM.

center upon the astrological symbolism employed throughout the work, as well as the fictional natural religion described in detail by its author.

2 Phillip Henry Gosse (1810-1888) was a naturalist and lay preacher who was known for encouraging the aquarium hobby as well as an attempt with his book *Omphalos* (1857) to reconcile the Biblical creation narrative with the theory of geologic ages.

3 Another piece of utopian daydreaming, James Harrington (1611-1677) produced *The Commonwealth of Oceana* in 1656, a political work enumerating the necessary qualities for a perfect republic.

4 Little is known about Pomponius Mela, other than his name and birthplace. A first-century Roman, Mela is responsible for an early work on geography, the aforementioned *De Situ Orbis* written around 43 A. D. Here, it is more difficult to argue against Machen's thesis as the book presents its subject rather dryly without the merest hint of occult mystery.

5 A third century writer, Gaius Julius Solinus used Mela's *De Situ Orbis* and Pliny's *Natural History* as source material to construct a picture of the ancient world in his work *De Mirabilibus Mundi*.

A READER OF CURIOUS BOOKS.

Vol. XI, March 1887, p.226-227

Sir,—My answer to Mr. Ingram's letter on the above subject, must, I fear, consist for the most part of apologies to the shade of Edgar A. Poe (let us hope no implacable one), and to Mr. Ingram himself, as Poe's "liege man of life and limb," sworn to defend him against all manner of folk. I unfortunately wrote without the "Tales of Mystery" on my desk; and, though I qualified one of my statements with an "I think," I do not wish in any way to palliate or glose over the very grave errors into which I fell.[6] In the first place, the title of Poe's tale was, as Mr. Ingram protests, incorrectly given; it is not "The Fall of the House of Ussher," with a double "s," but "The Fall of the House of Usher," with one "s." Secondly, I described Mr. Usher as delighting himself with the accounts of the "Mystic Dances of the Ægipans," whereas, as Mr. Ingram again protests, there is not one word of the "Mystic Dances of the Ægipans" in the story. The place of which I was thinking is as follows:—"and there were passages in Pomponius Mela about the old African Satyrs and Ægipans, over which Usher would sit dreaming for hours." Thirdly, Mr. Ingram denies that Mr. Gosse ever mentioned a work called "Ocean."[7] Neither did I, and this count I leave the shade of Harrington and the printer to settle between them, trusting again that even the angry ghosts of authors remember the line "The quality of mercy is not strained," &c.

But I am still of opinion that I have established my main contention; namely, that Poe, when he placed the works of Campanella and

6 Certainly, spelling errors may have slipped into the handling of Linotype tiles, but it seems rather unlikely that the printer would introduce an entire sentence, and one which produced so specific an error, into Machen's text. Furthermore, Machen makes no effort to offer an alternative to the supposedly alien line which seemed to agree so handsomely with Machen's argument.

7 The botching of Harrington's title (*Oceana*, not Ocean) shows further confusion. In this instance, Ingram fails to come away unscathed. Perhaps it is true that Gosse never mentioned a work entitled "Ocean" by another author. However, the naturalist did write his own book entitled *The Ocean* (1844).

Pomponius Mela on his mystic's shelves, was not aware of their real character. "Our books," he says . . . "were, as might be supposed, in strict keeping with this character of phantasm." Pomponius Mela and Campanella are not in strict keeping with this, or any other character of phantasm. Lastly, Mr. Ingram appears to believe that I intended to disparage the authors in question. Let us put the case that Poe had made Usher (with one "s") dream for hours over "Tristram Shandy" and "Pearson on the Creed,"[8] and that I, or any other man, had pointed out that neither of these works was "in strict keeping with this character of phantasm." Surely to do thus would be in nowise to disparage a rare humorist and a sound divine.

LEOLINUS

---

8 *The Life and Opinions of Tristam Shandy, Gentleman* (1759) is a satirical and bawdy novel by Laurence Sterne (1713-1768), an Anglican clergyman. *Exposition of the Creed* (1659) is a treatise on the Apostles' Creed by John Pearson, Bishop of Chester.

A READER OF CURIOUS BOOKS.

Vol. XI, April 1887, p.291

Sir,—Permit me in the first place to thank "Leolinus" for his courteous reply to my hasty note, and in the second to assure him that Edgar Poe did not publish remarks about books he was not conversant with. It is not possible for me at this moment to write a long article on Poe's intimate acquaintance with the curious works in the Usher Library, but if "Leolinus" will refer to "The Descent into the Maelstrom," or "The Island of the Fay," he will see that the maligned poet had not only a knowledge of Pomponius Mela's curious tome, but why he placed it amongst books of the class he did.[9]

JOHN HENRY INGRAM.

9 With regard to a segment on cosmological speculation, Poe inserted the following annotation to *The Island of the Fay*: "Speaking of the tides, Pomponius Mela, in his treatise *De Situ Orbis*, says 'either the world is a great animal,' or etc."

THE

FORTUNATE LOVERS;

OR,

Twenty-seven Novels of Marguerite, Queen of Navarre.

TRANSLATED FROM THE ORIGINAL FRENCH

BY

ARTHUR MACHEN.

*EDITED AND SELECTED FROM THE HEPTAMERON,
WITH NOTES & AN INTRODUCTION BY A. MARY F. ROBINSON,
AND ADORNED WITH A FRONTISPIECE BY
G. P. JACOMB HOOD.*

London :

GEORGE REDWAY, YORK STREET, COVENT GARDEN.

MDCCCLXXXVII.

Uisitation of the Monasteries
in the Reign of Henry the Eighth.

Vol. XI, February 1887, p.95-96

DURING the last ten or twenty years, scholars, and those interested in historical research, have become aware that the history of the so-called Reformation in the reigns of Henry, Edward, and Elizabeth has yet to be written. And with every fresh installment from the State Papers and other contemporary records, private and public, the impression grows in strength; and many of us begin to suspect that the "Glorious Reformation" must shortly take its place with the foundation of Rome by Romulus, William Tell's shooting of the arrow, the papacy of Joan, and other historical mirages. All who have read the volumes humorously called "Histories of England" are familiar with the scene painted in them, and the personages of the drama. We have as a dark background England, shrouded in an Egyptian night of ignorance and superstition—the Dark Ages, in short: which produced nevertheless Westminster Abbey, "La Morte d'Arthur," and the "Summa Theologiæ" of St. Thomas Aquinas. Against this gloomy background are relieved bishops, monks, and priests, all very wicked and dreadful persecutors; with an occasional Reformer or "Morning Star of the Reformation" of apostolic saintliness. Then enter Bluff King Hal, zealous Cromwell, conscientious Cranmer and the rest, who, aided by a loyal and Protestant people, all burning for the New Light and "a godly, thorough Reformation," make short work of the bad bishops and the evil monks, and all the abominations of the Scarlet Woman that sitteth upon the Seven Hills. Such was the picture, such the stories told to us in the Histories, and believed by most if not all. But now we begin to suspect that there is another side to the question; notably in the matter of the monks and their enormities; doubts are cast on King Hal's bluffness, Cromwell (some say) was a scoundrel, and Cranmer a syncophant and a time-server—an inflated Vicar of Bray. Mr. J. Gairdner has recently published his "Letters and Papers ... of the Reign of Henry VIII.," on which the *Athenæum* comments as follows:—

"Seldom in the world's history has a tyrant found baser instruments for his basest designs than Henry found for carrying out the visitation of the English monasteries. That there were foolish superstitions in some of the religious houses, that there were abuses in others—that some of the thousands among the inmates of monasteries, great and small, were living scandalous lives, and many more were living useless ones—nobody would be so silly as to deny. But that any monastery in England contained half a dozen such wretches as the more prominent of the visitors who came to despoil them is almost inconceivable. It is a sickening story. The reader of this volume, as he turns over page after page, is in danger of disbelieving everything that these men report, in his indignation at the audacious and manifest lying which characterises their reports. The men were not one whit better than common informers, and they never thought it worth while to deal with any but common informers. Runaway monks of blasted character, rogues who were on the look-out for a share of the spoil, fellows who were professional blacklegs, defaulters who had embezzled the convent's money and cooked their accounts, cowled ruffians who were actually confined in the prisons of the monasteries for their crimes—these and the like were the men to whom the visitors looked, and whose inventions they reported or even exaggerated."

The Seillière Library.

Vol. XI, February 1887, p.99-100

In the sixth chapter of the first part of "The Ingenious Gentleman Don Quixote de la Mancha" is contained the scrutiny of the Parson and the Barber, held in the library of Don Quixote; the results of which, it will be remembered, were more disastrous than any sale of our times. But "the first book that Master Nicholas gave into the parson's hands was Amadis de Gaul in four parts, and (said the parson) this seems to be a thing of mystery; for, according to what I have heard say, this was the first book of chivalry imprinted in Spain, and all the rest have drawn their beginning and origin from it; and so, according to my conceit, we should doom it to the fire without excuse, as the lawgiver to so ill a sect." Readers of the catalogue of the Seillière Library might be excused for thinking they had before them a list of Don Quixote's collection,[1] since it includes almost all the works criticised in the chapter we have cited, and will doubtless tempt collectors to wish the precious volumes could by some means be enchanted into their possession. The library, a portion of which will be sold by auction, on the 28th of this month (February) and four following days, by Messrs. Sotheby, Wilkinson & Hodge, was formed by the late Baron Seillière, and amongst the romances we may mention the following:—

Hystoire du Noble Roy Ponthus, Lyon, 1480;
Isaie le Triste, Paris, s.d.;
Percival le Galloys, 1530;
Les Quatre Fils d'Aymon, Lyon, 1480;
Tirant lo Blanch, Valencia, 1490;
Roman de la Rose, the first, and several other early editions;
Bertrand du Gusclin, Lyon, vers 1485;
Tyturell und Parzival of Wolfram von Eschenbach, 1477;
Cronica del Cid, Burgos, 1512; Palmerin de Oliva, 1526;

---

1 To review *Don Quixote*, Part I, Chapter 6, which references some of these titles, refer to the Appendices section, page 101.

Amadis de Gaula, 1508, the only copy known, and numerous other editions in Spanish, French, Italian, and German;
Ly Romans de Vraye Amour, MS., sœc. sixteenth; Historia de Don Polindo, Toledo, 1526;
L'Arbre de Batailles, MS. of the fifteenth century, and also the almost unique first edition of the same book, 1477;
Artus de Bretaigne, s.d.;
Tewrdanckh, Augsb., 1519;
Enzina, Cancionero, Caragoça, 1516;
Champion des Dames, Lyon, s.d.;
L'Histoire du Sainct-Greal, 1523;
Valentin et Orson, Lyon, 1505;
Hug Shæpler, Strasburg, 1500;
Les Neuf Preux, Abbeville, 1487;
El Cavallero Florisandro, Salamanca, 1510;
Lancelot du Lac, 1533;
Meliadus de Leonnoys, 1532;

and lastly, there is the *editio princeps* of Don Quixote, Madrid, 1605, the knight being for once in knightly company.[2]

2 Machen reports on the results of this sale in the News and Notes section of the June issue: "The great battle of the Seillière sale was fought between Mr. Quaritch and Mr. Ellis over the black-letter folio (Valencia, 1490), Tirant lo Blanch. Mr. Quaritch eventually became the purchaser for £605. Two other copies of this edition are known to exist, one being in the Grenville Collection, and the other in the library of Valencia University."

𝔄 𝔏𝔬𝔰𝔱 𝔚𝔬𝔯𝔨.

February 1887, pp. 100-101

Disraeli, in his "Curiosities of Literature,"[1] gives an amusing account of a book entitled *De Tribus Impostoribus*.[2] "The Duke de la Vallière, and the Abbé de St. Leger once concerted together to supply the eager purchaser of literary rarities with a copy of *De Tribus Impostoribus*, a book, by the date, pretended to have been printed in 1598, though probably a modern forgery of 1698. The title of such a work had long existed by rumour, but never was a copy seen by man; works printed with this title being proved to be modern fabrications. A copy, however, of the *introuvable* original was sold at the Duke de la Vallière's sale. The history of this volume is curious. The Duke and the Abbé having manufactured a text, had it printed in the old Gothic character, under the title *De Tribus Impostoribus*. They proposed to put the great bibliopolist, De Bure, in good humour, whose agency would sanction the imposture. They were afterwards to dole out copies at twenty-five louis each—a reasonable price for a book which no one had ever seen. They invited De Bure to dinner, flattered and cajoled him, and at a moment when, as they imagined, they had wound him up to their pitch, they exhibited their manufacture. The keen-eyed glance of the renowned cataloguer of the 'Bibliographie Instructive' instantly shot like lightning over it, and like lightning destroyed the whole edition." So far Disraeli; but in the *Religio Medici* Sir Thomas Browne says—"That villain and secretary of hell that composed that miscreant piece of the 'Three Impostors,' though divided from all religions, and was neither Jew,

---

1 A noted bibliophile, Isaac Disraeli (1766-1848) is most famous for being the father of Prime Minister Benjamin Disraeli. Machen's excerpt comes from a chapter entitled "Literary Forgeries" from *Curiosities of Literature, Volume III* according to the reckoning of the 1824 edition. Disraeli's work made a lasting impression on Machen who wrote fondly on it nearly fifty years later in the essay *Tom O'Bedlam and His Song* (1930).

2 Despite its notorious reputation, there is no evidence for the existence of this legendary text, sometimes known as the *Treatise of the Three Impostors*, which accuses the founders of the three great Abrahamic faiths to be frauds. It was first referenced

Turk, nor Christian, was not a positive Atheist."[3] Now Sir Thomas Browne, writing about 1635, cannot be speaking of the Vallière forgery of 1698; he must therefore have seen either the genuine "Three Impostors," or else a forgery of very early date. Can any of the readers of THE ANTIQUARIAN throw any light on this curious piece of literary history; or must the "Three Impostors" take their places beside Junius, the Eikon Basilike,[4] and other veiled obscurities?[5]

in the tenth century and has been the subject of hoaxes well into the eighteenth. Machen later appropriated the title for his excellent novel: "...I liked the sound of the title, and noted it in '85, and indicated in my notebook the sort of book—a picaresque romance—I should like to write under that head; and so had the title waiting for me in the spring of 1895." (Danielson, 1923.) In this case, the "three impostors" are members of a deadly occult group operating in *fin de siècle* London.

3 Highly influential, Sir Thomas Brown (1605-1682) authored books in a number of fields including science and religion, including *Religio Medici* (1643). Here, Machen assumes that Browne had literally examined the supposed treatise, but that is rather unlikely. The "villain and secretary of hell" is Bernardino Ochino (1487-1564) a Protestant reformer who carried controversial views on religious matters including Unitarianism, divorce, and possibly, polygamy. Brownes's assertion that he was the author of such a scandalous text may be a result of rumor borne out of Ochino's poor reputation, or perhaps a rhetorical device against his ideas.

4 Junius refers to an anonymous writer who published polemical letters in the Daily Post and Advertiser between January 1769 to January 1772. *Eikon Basilike* (1649) was published shortly after the execution of King Charles I, later canonized as a martyr by the Church of England. Though presented as an autobiography, authorship has never been conclusively proven.

5 A response to this query was not recorded in the pages of the magazine.

The Vision of William concerning Piers the Plowman;
together with Richard the Redeless.

March 1887, pp. 205-206

William Langland is said to have worked for twenty years in the forging of his Vision; and at last he has found an editor no less laborious than himself. In the first of these two handsome volumes, the student of our early literature will find the three texts, A, B, and C, with the various readings noted at the foot of each page. The second volume contains a preface, notes, and glossary; and it is here that the antiquarian and lettered man will revel in what is to them a Rabelaisian banquet of ancient lore. But, amidst the mazes of an orthography and a syntax which look strangely to the modern English eye, it is curious to find such expressions as "Ded as a dore-nayle" and "The newest thing out," and many others of like formation. In "Piers the Plowman" is related the fable of the rats and mice trying to bell the cat; the rats being the burgesses and more influential men among the commons, the mice, those of less importance; while the cat is Edward III., and the kitten his son Richard. Professor Skeat considers that the true dialect of the poem is found in text B; namely, a dialect chiefly Midland, with occasional introduction of southern forms. We give the following note as an example of Professor Skeat's method: —

"*Purnele* or *Peronelle* (from Petronilla) was a proverbial name for a gaily dressed bold-faced woman. May 31 was dedicated to St. Petronilla the Virgin; she was supposed to be able to cure the quartan ague. The name, once common, now scarcely survives, except as a surname in the form of Parnell."

And again, in etymology, on the word *nonechenche*:—

"This is the modern *nuncheon*; and the spelling shows that the derivation is from *none*, noon, and *schenche*, a pouring out or dispensing of drink, from A.-S. *scencan*, to pour out drink, to skink. Similarly the provincial English *nammut* luncheon, is *noon-meat*."

Finally, this is a work which all modern representatives of the "Clerke of Oxenford" should have at their "beddes head," though it is not "y-clothed in blake and red," but in a grave and decent surcoat of dark blue.

THE MEDIÆVAL CELLARER.

Ⓣⓗⓔ Ⓒⓤⓡⓘⓞⓢⓘⓣⓘⓔⓢ ⓞⓕ Ⓐⓛⓔ.

April 1887, pp. 229-232

It is clear that Æschylus the Athenian had but a poor opinion of the virtues of ale; at all events, in his "Supplices" we find a character thus expressing himself:—

"But the stout inmates of this brave old land
Ye will not find ale-bibbers."

The "brave old land" in question is Egypt; and with Egypt Mr. Bickerdyke begins his Institutes of Ale. Four thousand years ago, if the records "hid under Egypt's pyramid" lie not, the land of the Nile was convulsed by a kind of Local Option movement, which resulted in a wholesale closing of beer-shops. Truly "the thing that hath been, it is that which shall be," but beer-shops, so far, seem in no peril of becoming extinct. Mr. Bickerdyke makes but the brief stay of a paragraph in Egypt, and before long we find ourselves in Mediæval England, the happy hunting-ground of the antiquarian. Divers weighty questions have to be propounded, and, if possible, resolved. A kind of beery mist rises like a veil before us, into which we peer, and vainly endeavour to discern the date of the bringing in of hops. In a letter of donations under the hand of the great King Pepin we find mention of a "humularia," or hop-gardens, and it seems probable that hops were known, though not generally used, in Saxon times. Naturally there is a good deal about the regular clergy, commonly called "the old monks," who have somehow acquired the reputation of being Pantagruelists before Pantagruel. However that maybe, it seems certain that they had a great reverence for ale, and were sticklers for their daily allowance, requiring both quality and quantity to be above suspicion, or perhaps we should say, above proof. Awful legends are told in the monastic annals concerning the turpitude of one Roger Norreys, known as "The Wicked Abbot of Evesham." His monks bore with him and his sins for some while, but at last, on his compelling them "to drink ale little stronger than water," they revolted, and petitioned the Archbishop. Roger, however, seems to have taken good care to drink of the strong himself, and resembled in this point the abbot of the rhyme:

> "Bonum vinum cum sapore
> Bibit Abbas cum Priore,
> Sed conventus de pejore
>   Semper solet bibere."

The old maxim was that the cellarer "Pater debet esse totius congregationis"—should be the father of the whole convent; a touching proof of the high estimate in which the office was held. Full particulars are given in this admirable work of the exact allowance of ale served out to the monks, both on ordinary days and on the high days when everybody was busily engaged in "doing the great O"—that is, nothing. Next we have the witness of the poets concerning ale, from the author of "Piers the Plowman," Chaucer, and Taylor, the water poet, to the nameless quire of ballad-makers. Their testimony may be summed up in the words of one of them:—

> "Mas Mault he is a gentleman,
> And hath been since the world began;
> Never yet knew I any man
> That could match with Master Mault."

The various species of Church ales furnish Mr. Bickerdyke with another topic. These Church ales seem to have been a very sensible method of raising money, and appear in the main to have been free from scandal. In the seventeenth century, however, "some melancholy swains" persuaded the English people that—

> "The morrice-idols, Whitsun-ales can be
> But prophane reliques of a jubilee."

They passed away therefore, like many a goodly old observance, from the English life, but are still dear to the antiquary's heart. In reading Mr. Bickerdyke's book we are often moved to sigh over the degenerate days in which we live. Take, for instance, this list of the contents of a gentleman's cellar in the twelfth century: "In promptuario sive in celario sunt cadi, utres, dolea, ciphi, vina, scicera, cervicia, mustum, claretum, nectar, medo sive ydromellum, piretum, vinum rosetum, vinum falernum, vinum girofilatum." What gentleman could now refresh his guest with a glass of "vinum girofilatum?" Too often we fear, in these days of reduced rents, the list might stand thus: "In celario sunt cadi," all serving merely to illustrate the lines:—

"Quo semel est imbuta recens servabit odorem
Testa diu."

And what would have been said by the Dissenters if 300 tuns of ale, 100 tuns of wine, and "one pynt of hypocrass" had been consumed at the enthronement of the Archbishop of Canterbury? Yet in the days of Edward IV., a mere Archbishop of York thus entertained his guests. Much curious lore has been gathered and stored in these "Curiosities" on the matter of signs. Firstly we have the bush (which good wine needs not), then the ale-stake, or ale-pole, and lastly the painted or figured sign, sometimes seen combined with the primitive bush. The most elaborate sign on record is that of the White Hart at Norwich, mentioned by Sir Thomas Brown in 1663. It was made in 1655, and is said to have cost £1,000. There were on it "a great many stories as of Charon and Cerberus, Actaeon and Diana," and this masterpiece of carved and painted work remained undestroyed till the end of the last century. A poor wit; a member of the "shoe-black seraph" gild of authors, was once staying at the White Horse, on the old Bath road, and having (we may safely assume) eaten of the fat and drunken of the strong, had to spend such another quarter of an hour as that memorable in Rabelaisian story. But the landlord was generous and forgave the author his score, and he, in return, wrote large beneath the sign (naming other inns in the neighbourhood):—

"My White Horse shall beat (bait ?) the Bear,
    And make the Angel fly;
Shall turn the Ship quite bottom-up,
    And drink the Three Cups dry."

By the kindness of Messrs. Field & Tuer we are able to give two of the cuts which quaintly adorn "The Curiosities of Ale and Beer," and our readers may rest assured, that if these but meagrely represent the illustrations, our remarks do scarcely more justice to the letterpress. The *Athenæum*, in reviewing the work, declared that it ought to have been dedicated to "the most noble and illustrious tosspots and thrice precious profligates" of Rabelais' Prologue; and so say we, for these "Curiosities" are "fair, goodly books, stuffed with high conceptions."

Arthur Machen

The Blood Covenant.

April 1887, pp. 276-277

The covenant, or solemn pact, made both between man and man, and between man and God, seems in most instances, and in most ages, to have been symbolised by the pouring forth of blood. In the words of the Bible, "The blood is the life," the soul of a man (*psyche*, not *pneuma*); and it is an open question in physiological science, whether the ancient belief of blood transference being also soul-transference is not, in a measure, true; for there are instances on record of insanity having been cured by the transfusion of blood. Dr. Trumbull has with diligent care traced the history of the covenant in blood through the various races and ages of mankind. In the Egyptian "Book of the Dead," or "Book of the Going Forth into Day," "Osiris opens the turning door," the gateway of light, "by the covenant of the blood-giving arm." In Salvator Rosa's picture of the Conspiracy of Catiline, "Two conspirators stand face to face, their right hands clasped above a votive altar. The bare right arm of each is incised, the blood is streaming from the arm of one into a cup which he holds to receive it; while the dripping arm of the other conspirator shows that his blood has already flowed into the commingling cup." At the present day in Syria persons who wish to bind each other by the most sacred ties of friendship, exchange blood, and are known henceforth "as Brothers of the Covenant." Such a relationship is considered a closer one than any ordinary brotherhood. Mr. H. M. Stanley has covenanted thus with fifty African chiefs, from Mirambo who is lord of 90,000 square miles of territory, downwards; and in Arabic the same word ('alaq) means "love" and "blood." Among the Kayans of Borneo the covenant is observed, and in a curious fashion. The blood is taken from the contracting parties and spread on a cigar or cigarette, which is then smoked by the two men, who are now brothers in blood. A curious reason is assigned for the selection of the ring- finger in the marriage ceremony, namely, that a very delicate nerve was believed to run from the finger in question to the heart, and so not only hands but hearts and life were thus bound together.

Dr. Trumbull's work is furnished with an appendix and indices, and will be valued by students of anthropology and theology, and even by those idle, short-gowned students who love the blind alleys, quaint courts, and dim by-ways of knowledge.

Christopher Marlowe.

May 1887, pp. 334-335

This edition of Tamburlaine, Doctor Faustus, The Jew of Malta, and Edward the Second, forms the first volume of "The Mermaid Series," in which the publishers promise to include all "the best plays of the old dramatists." The title of the series is one of pleasant promise; as if we were to be taken to that rare old tavern and to hear once more the choice conceits of Ben and his sons, and forerunners. And, if we may judge from the present volume, this promise will be fulfilled; and students with all lovers of literature will have cause to bless the Mermaid and her treasure. To Marlowe, who has been chosen as the first "old dramatist" to be edited, high praise is undoubtedly due for it was Marlowe who first wrote musical blank verse, and made it "easily an art." Scattered about his plays, amidst a good deal of bombast, or something perilously like it, are lines and passages of extreme loveliness; in short, Marlowe at his best is unsurpassed. The editing of the book seems on the whole satisfactory; archaic words are explained, various readings given, and occasionally critical passages from Mr. Swinburne and other authorities are quoted in the foot-notes. At the end of the work we are presented with the bill of accusation brought against Marlowe by "one Richard Bame." He was charged by Richard Bame with holding "damnable opinions," and we think Richard was judicious in his use of epithets. We are glad to hear that Messrs. Vizetelly & Co have cancelled these last pages in the second edition of "Christopher Marlowe."

DOLMEN, NEAR HESHBON.

Syrian Stone-Lore.

May 1887, pp. 335-336

With the early Turanian[1] family of man—and particularly with that branch of it called Kheta or Hittites—Captain Conder begins his "Syrian Stone-Lore." Of this people our knowledge till recent times was slight, but the researches of scholars and explorers have done a good deal to remove the archæology of the Hittites from the dim and debatable land of conjecture. Thus we know that they lived in a country full of towns, that they had horses and chariots like the Amaur (probably the Amorites), that their complexion was lighter than that of the Semitic tribes, that they wore pigtails of a Chinese appearance, and boots. They were, in fact, a tribe of Tatars, worshipping (as Captain Conder's latest discoveries prove) the sun, the moon, the wind, rain, and the like powers of nature. But from an early date these Turanian Hittites seemed to have shared the land with Semitic peoples; mostly, indeed, the Hittites were the overlords and the superiors in civilisation of the Perizzites, Hivites, Jebusites, &c., all of whom came of the Semitic stock. The Phœnicians were from the first the traders of Palestine. Their religious ideas were, to a large extent, phallic, and one of their talismans was the Red Hand,[2] to this day a charm in Syria under the name of Kef Miriam, the "Virgin Mary's Hand." It may be noted that Captain Conder considers the Egyptian Ankh, or emblem of life, to be a representation of the "holy and shining tree of Asshur," and not a phallic emblem. It is curious that the legend of Melusina may be traced, we dare not say to its source, in Phoenician Mythology,

1   From an anthropological perspective, Turanian has been used in reference to peoples of Central Asia. However, Machen would later appropriate the term as a description for the Little People. From this standpoint, aspects of fairy-lore represented an inherited memory for an ancient race who inhabited Britain before the arrival of the Celts.

2   It is interesting to suppose that this forgotten book provided imagery to one of Machen's most effective horror stories. Published in 1895, *The Red Hand* dealt with punishment administered by Machen's Turanian-inspired Little People. The namesake symbol is left prominently at the scene of the crime.

in which the husband of the Serpent Princess is the Phœnician Hercules. To this day many Phœnician customs are preserved by the Neapolitans, who sometimes leap through a fire shouting, "Bel, Bel!" and, like the Phœnicians, are accustomed to paint eyes on the prows of their boats. Passing to the Hebrews, we note that all Captain Conder's research goes to prove the substantial accuracy of the Old Testament history. For instance: "The names, Moses, Putiel, Gersom, and Phinehas appear to be Egyptian, as is possibly also that of Aaron, a strong argument in favour of their historic reality." It is satisfactory also to have Captain Conder's declaration that "the theories which recognise the 'lost tribes' in Afghans or American Indians (we might add, or in Englishmen) are not founded on any real scientific, ethnological, or antiquarian information." But such theories have proved to be wonderfully attractive to the weaker brethren. Thus, from age to age, and from race to race, the author gives the history of Syria, as he has read it on stone, on coin, and tile tablet. We have not so much as indicated a tithe of the field covered by Captain Conder. The Byzantine period is, perhaps of all, the most interesting, being in comparative darkness, and, as it were, out of the highways of history. And it is in the byways that the antiquarian is most fain to walk. By the kindness of Messrs. Bentley & Son we are able to give our readers a specimen of the many illustrations which increase the interest of Captain Conder's work. Very few of these dolmens remain in the country to westward of the Jordan, the explanation of this fact being that the Jewish kings Hezekiah and Josiah destroyed, as far as they were able, all the religious emblems of the Canaanites. But such structures, where they exist, are held in awe and honour by the modern Bedawîn, who style them "Ghouls' Houses."

Phantasms of the Living.

May 1887, pp. 343-345

In these large volumes, one of nearly 600 and the other of more than 700 pages, the earnest and distinguished members of the Society for Psychical Research whose names are given above, embody the results of prolonged and laborious exertions, the purpose of which cannot be easily defined. The contents of their book may be described readily enough. It consists of an enormous collection of anecdotes, verified with great care, relating to cases in which impressions have been conveyed from one mind to another by channels which are not those of the ordinary physical senses. Sometimes these transfers of thought have been experimental, sometimes "spontaneous." In the latter cases they have often had to do with visions, seen at a distance, of persons on the point of death. But the authors do not present us with these facts as proof of anything beyond their bare existence as facts. No one can say they are unimportant facts, but they are only important really, if they lead somewhere, and the authors seem almost anxious to crush every hypothesis which would lend them this sort of value. The book is a monument of painstaking care, devoted to the preparation of its materials, the arrangement and codification of its contents. In reference, for instance, to one prolonged series of trials in connection with the thought transference of numbers we read:—"The probability which this result affords for a cause other than chance is represented by forty-seven nines and a 5 following a decimal point; that is the odds are nearly two hundred thousand million trillions of trillions to 1." But still the 1,300 pages of the book are all practically devoted to fortifying this conclusion, namely, the fact of "telepathy," or thought transference. The authors not only do not go further themselves, they are resolute in resisting the further passage of anyone else. Other writers on psychological mysteries have often, no doubt, been open to the reproach that they were over ready to be convinced. Messrs. Gurney and Myers seem, on the contrary, to covet above all things the reputation of being the Major Bagstocks of psychic research "devilish sly!"—amateur detectors in regions of inquiry, with which they do not sympathise. They are not content to assure the world of the truth of the one or two theories they are inclined to espouse. They are still eager to convince us that no one else has any right to go further than they do. This attitude of mind seems to have limited the scope of their work, until its value is reduced to very small proportions. The phenomena of consciousness must remain what so many physical scientists apparently think them to be—an uninteresting region of research—unless they hinge on to conjectures concerning a future life. The present history of phantasms will only serve to irritate without enlightening materialists, unless the conclusions they suggest go a great deal beyond the point to which they are carried by the society that might now almost be called the Psychical Inquisition. Mr. Myers has done something no doubt in laying down a foundation in minds of the most materialistic order, on which other writers may build later on. But, even as regards this relatively humble though useful work, he seems to make the mistake of arguing as if even the people who have long been fully convinced of his conclusions were not entitled to believe even what he now teaches, before he and his friends had docketed the reasons now found to justify such belief, and had certified them as fit for consumption. This impatience of researches differing from their own, so oddly united with a disposition to cross a little beyond the conventional boundaries of materialism, seems in compatible with the breadth of view one might have expected to find associated with such an undertaking as that embodied in the volumes before us.

Again, in preparing such a monumental work as this, personal animosity ought to have been eliminated. The cult which some call Esoteric Buddhism and others call Theosophy should have been let severely alone. In an otherwise powerful introduction, however, Mr. Myers exhibits the almost comical vanity of supposing that, because "acting through Mr. Hodgson," the society he represents came to a conclusion unfavourable to the "claim of the so-called Theosophy of which Madame Blavatsky was the prophetess," therefore the "loudly vaunted evidence" for its marvels has crumbled away. That seems a matter of opinion, and nothing is more certain than that, under whatever name it flourishes, this cult is making steady progress, not only in this country, but on the Continent, in America, and India, and even in Australia. And it is noteworthy that the class which is attracted by the studies suggested in works like those of Mr. Sinnett, of Colonel Olcott, of Dr. Anna Kingsford, and of Mr. Laurence Oliphant, is the class which reads the most, travels the most, converses the most, and thinks the most, a class by no means likely to be seriously imposed upon. It is unwise to assume, as Messrs. Myers and Gurney do in these volumes, that, because a friend of theirs, a Mr. Hodgson, ventured an attack on the author of "Isis Unveiled," which has since been the subject of animated controversy, the theosophical movement has been crushed out of existence. Indeed, such a case would only go to prove that Esoteric Buddhism had previously thriven solely on the support of the S. P. R., and this would be an absurd proposition, as Messrs. Myers and Gurney will be the first to admit. Though blemished in this way by a narrow-minded and prejudiced spirit, the great work on Phantasms ought now to put some of the first principles of psychic science on a new foundation for the whole intellectual world. Of course, however, it has not yet done so. If *The Times* or The *Athenæum* to-morrow had to mention "thought transference," or the theory that the vision of a dying person could be seen at a distance, those orthodox journals would be bound, by their allegiance to the prevalent belief of the majority, to assume an air of more or less polite or contemptuous incredulity, the politeness or contempt varying with the social standing of the persons concerned. But this is due to deeper characteristics of human nature than any of those even to which Mr. Myers and Mr. Gurney have yet directed their ingenious experiments. For some sorts of belief, minds must be trained to receive the evidence which lead up to it before such evidence can have any practical effect on their intellectual growth, however complete it may be in itself. Where our authors get an appreciative hearing, their audiences have thus been developed. Perhaps their own inability to assimilate evidence which presents itself as a revelation to others, may be due to an inverted application of the same principle.

The Influence of Italian
upon English Literature.

June 1887, pp. 418-419

Mr. J. Ross Murray's pleasantly written sketch puts into a concise form the principal features of the debt owed to Italy by our great dramatists and poets of the sixteenth and seventeenth centuries. It is unfortunate that the prescribed limits of the essay (which obtained the Le Bas prize in 1885) prevented the author from dwelling upon the interesting subject of the obligations of Chaucer, and of some even of the popular balladists, to Italian originals; but over the ground he has covered we may safely follow him. As a chronicler of facts, he does not go into the subtler of those causes which lay at the root of the peculiarly seductive faculty of Italian letters. We may observe any day that the study of Italian authors has a more forming effect upon the intellectual taste than the study of the rich and varied literatures of France and Germany. People, again, who have read much Italian, generally write their own language with a certain ease and elegance which is scarcely the outcome of extensive reading of French or German; and our grandmothers, who were commonly good Italian scholars, had a *non so che* of literary refinement which is not invariably present in their far better informed descendants.

While fully recognising the intellectual worth of the treasures imported from Italy, Mr. Murray is strong in his condemnation of the moral ideas which slipped in at the same time; nor is he, perhaps, too severe, except when he associates Tasso with those writers whose aim was simply to amuse, and "who were not very careful about any other end." This seems rather hard on the poet of the *Gerusalemme* and the *Mondo Creato*. The latter poem might, by the bye, have been mentioned in connection with "Paradise Lost," some passages in which display an almost certain familiarity with Tasso's last work.

The Trade Signs of Essex.

June 1887, pp. 419-420

Many of our readers, while passing through the dim and narrow streets of an old English town, have doubtless noticed the mysterious blazonry known as "The Chequers," painted mostly on the door-post, and often in need of a fresh coat of colour. To many "The Chequers" is a riddle and an enigma; but let such hear Mr. Christy:—"It is said to be found even among the ruins of Pompeii," but "Larwood and Hotten say that in England it represents the coat of arms of the Earls de Warrenne and Surrey, who bore *Chequy, or and azure*, and in the reign of Edward IV. possessed the privilege of licensing ale-houses. The old money-changers used boards, divided up into squares like a modern chess-board, and the sign of the Chequers may have originated, partly, at least, in these 'exchequers,' as they were called, being hung up outside their places of business. Not improbably the sign also represents the 'Chequer,' or board divided into squares, and still used in some country inns for keeping a tally or record of the amount drunk by each regular customer." With such curious information "The Trade Signs of Essex" abounds, and Mr. Christy has so admirably methodised his subject-matter, that the student is able to refer easily to any species of sign. There are signs Heraldic, Mammalian, Ornithological, Reptilian, Botanical, Human, Nautical, and Astronomical; and best of all Miscellaneous. The "Chequers" is miscellaneous, so is "The Crooked Billett," which turns out to be a *fess dancette* or *chevron*, and so also is "The Leather Bottle," concerning which Mr. Christy cites a communication of Mr. T. B. Daniell:—"My father recollects a veritable leather bottle being purchased at a sale by his father. It was a cylindrical belt of black leather, very stout, with two circular ends (also of leather) sewn in, a double thickness of the same material over the bung-hole (which received a cork for stopper), and a short strap to carry it by. Its capacity was about a gallon." The book is full of illustrations, some of them being reproductions from old prints; the frontispiece, for instance, shows "Chelmsford High Street in 1760." There is a glossary of heraldic terms, and a full and accurate index.

NOY'S HOUSE IN BRENTFORD.

June 1887, pp. 435

Sir,— Some of your readers may have seen the old house in the main street of Brentford which is reputed to have been the residence of Noy, Attorney-General to Charles I. It is a mediæval building of the usual type, and had a "barge-board" of good and bold design. Passing through the town some few weeks ago, I was astonished to find that this curious barge-board had been violently torn away. Can anyone inform me when, and for what cause, this outrage was perpetrated?[1]

Cosmopoli.

LEOLINUS

1 It does not appear that Machen's query was answered in the pages of *Walford's Antiquarian.*

La Vie Privée d'autrefois :
Arts et Métiers, Modes, Mœurs, Usages des Parisiens du xiie au xviiie Siècle.

July 1887, pp. 44-46

One of the most amusing specimens of antiquarian literature which the Paris presses have lately produced is undoubtedly M. Alfred Franklin's work, "La Vie Privée de nos Pères." Two volumes of this series are now before us, containing a fund of curious information, and, if the forthcoming installments are of the like nature, we can promise to our readers a rare treat in the way of humour, and, at the same time, of picturesque details of the private life of our forefathers between the twelfth and the eighteenth centuries. We say *our* forefathers, because, although the scene of these volumes is laid in Paris, the manners and customs of the "good old times" were pretty much alike on both sides of the Channel.

Let us deal, in the first place, with advertisements, bills, notices, and puffs of every kind. M. Alfred Franklin calls the nineteenth century *le siècle de la réclame*, and he is perfectly right. There is nothing absolutely faultless in this sublunary world, and therefore the famous compositions of the late George Robins, the prose and poetical announcements extolling the merits of Rowland's Odonto and Mrs. Allen's hair-restorer may have some flaw in them; but, as our author truly observes, a tradesman knows within a little what profit he can reckon upon by not hiding his light under a bushel, and it is not too much to say that even literary criticism is now supplanted by puff carried to its last state of perfection. Some readers may perhaps find no small comfort in discovering that the science of advertising is as early as the thirteenth century, and Etienne Boileau's "Livre des Métiers" contains strict injunctions against those merchants who depreciated the goods of their neighbours in order to secure a sale for their own. M. Franklin gives us interesting particulars on the structure, the conveniences, and management of the Paris shops; he shows us the public criers filling the place now occupied by bills, posters, and the advertisement sheets of newspapers; and, not satisfied with quoting from the doggerel of Jehan de Garlande and Guillaume de Villeneuve many a passage illustrating the noisy appearance of the streets of the French metropolis, he reprints at the end of the volume the "Crieries de Paris" of the latter, and several pieces of the same character. Nothing was deemed worth purchasing which was not announced with all the ceremony that could be procured, and, as a case in point, we would refer our readers to M. Franklin's narrative of the fuss which took place whenever a ship freighted with foreign wines arrived at the Place de Grève. The town solicitor, the clerk to the provost, and a couple of officers, wrote down an inventory of the precious cargo, sealed the casks, and fixed the prices. This once done, the public criers, with napkins fastened round their neck, holding a pot in one hand and a goblet in the other, went through all the streets and royal "hotels" announcing the important arrival, and recommending to thirsty customers the nectar of Beaune, Grenache, Chablis, Epernay, and Burgundy. Wine, of course, suggests glasses; itinerant vendors carrying that brittle article could be met with at almost every corner, providing, at a cheap rate, small wares for ladies and tumblers for the use of the regular tipplers. The middle ages saw the rule of monopolies and the tyranny of corporate bodies; M. Franklin gives plenty of instances of the abuse which such a system led to.

The laws of cleanliness and of *savoir-vivre* form the subject of the second volume, a rather extensive and complicated one as we may imagine, for it begins with bathing-places and hair-dressers, goes on with tailoring and millinery, and takes due account of politeness and manners. The barbers were generally surgeons and bath-proprietors as well (*chirurgiens-barbiers-étuvistes*), nor did they refuse, in cases of need, to perform dangerous operations. This last quality, however, was attended with so many accidents that in 1637 Louis XIII. authorised the creation of a new corporation, namely that of the *barbiers-barbants*, who were expressly prohibited from practising surgery. Against this innovation a protest was entered on the part of the *barbiers-chirurgiens*, and the edict originated by the son of Henry IV. could not be carried out before 1673.

M. Franklin informs us that the Parisians of the seventeenth century "neglected the most elementary requirements of cleanliness; they had nearly completely lost the habit of washing. . . . The Church considered that habit as a dangerous usage, an objectionable piece of vanity, a sin. As a rule monks bathed only twice a year, at Christmas and at Easter. The statutes of Saint Benedict thus express themselves: 'Invalids shall be allowed the use of baths when ever it is deemed necessary; but to those who are in the enjoyment of good health, especially if they are young, permission must be granted only seldom (*sanis autem, et maxime juvenibus, tardius concedatur*).'" Dom Calmet informs us that each Benedictine monk had a comb of his own, and that they combed their hair and washed their faces *pretty often*.

From these details we can gather that our ancestors paid very little attention to manners; the use of pocket-handkerchiefs was not deemed essential amongst even gentlefolk, and those who did indulge in that luxury practised it on artistic principles. Even as late as 1797, de la Mésangère said: "A few years ago blowing one's nose had become an art. One imitated the sound of a trumpet, another the screaming of a cat. The point of perfection consisted in making neither too much noise nor too little."

Hair powder is another branch of toilet which receives its due notice in M. Franklin's book; the popularity it obtained seems wonderful to us, and we are astonished at seeing it described as an evidence of advanced civilisation. During the few years which preceded the Revolution, the professed philanthropists eloquently bemoaned the waste of flour used for powdering the hair, whilst the whole population of France was threatened with starvation.

From what we have thus said it would be a mistake to suppose that the two volumes for which we are indebted to M. Franklin are merely a collection of anecdotes without any importance or value. They illustrate, on the contrary, history in the most signal manner, and afford us interesting and trustworthy light on the social and domestic usages of times long gone by. Woodcuts copied from old prints have been plentifully added, and each volume is completed by an appendix, the perusal of which is specially reserved and recommended to scholars, whereas it is of too light a character for general reading.

The Marriage of Cupid and Psyche.

August 1887, pp. 110-111

The custom of printing small *éditions de luxe* of works (either original or reprints) of archæological or traditional interest is one which deserves hearty commendation: "it blesseth him that gives and him that takes," for surely an author or editor can have no sweeter satisfaction than that of viewing his intellectual offspring or foster child dressed in such beautiful Sunday clothes. The other day it was Professor Child who sent across the Atlantic one of those agreeable booklets, "The Childe of Bristowe," admirably modernised by himself. Now it is Mr. Andrew Lang who gives us, folded in vellum and imprinted in a type which would not have done discredit to an Aldine, a monograph on the ever-charming folk-tale (as he proves it to be) of Cupid and Psyche, with Adlington's translation from the text of Apuleius, not to speak of two or three choice etchings and designs, and some scraps of verse, of which it need only be said that they are fit flowers to grow in such a garden of delight. Mr. Lang's essay is an able exposition of his well-known views on the Spontaneous Generation of popular stories, or at least, their universal prevalence in opposition to the theory which would refer the origin of nearly all European tales to an identical Indian source. He mentions, incidentally, that the story of Cupid and Psyche is in substance the same as that of Beauty and the Beast—a statement which has called forth this graceful protest from the pen of Mr. W. H. Pollock:—

The Folklorist, it is one's bounden duty,
If not to cherish, to consult at least;
But, though I'm sure that Psyche was a *Beauty*,
I cannot think that Cupid was a *Beast*.

Palæolithic Man in N.W. Middlesex.

August 1887, pp. 111-112

Matters relating to the unknown have always an attraction; so that anything tending to throw additional light on the history of Palæolithic man is certain, on that account alone, to be of interest, not only to the "prehistoric" Antiquary, but even to the general reader. In this little work Mr. Allen Brown has described certain worked flints obtained by him from the drift gravels of the Ealing district in a manner which lends additional interest to a subject so absorbing and attractive as the rude stony relics of a long lost and unknown race. Of course, such implements have already been described by other workers from other parts of the great Thames valley area, and the old deposits of the sea, Medway, &c.; but the manner in which the author of "Palæolithic Man in N.W. Middlesex" treats his subject, gives it a charm of interest and value which will be much appreciated by the student, as well as by those who have hitherto read nothing whatever of the subject. In the first place Mr. Allen Brown, instead of dropping at once into what would be to many an abstruse subject, leads the reader through the archæological, geological, and physical aspects of the early history of man, and thus prepares him for the description of his discoveries in the old Ealing gravels. His references to numerous well-known authors on this subject are copious and well selected; and those to the works of travellers and explorers are also of great value, and will be of service to the Ethnological student who may wish to peruse works bearing on the objects of his research. Mr. Allen Brown also throws much additional interest into his subject by drawing numerous comparisons between the worked flints of Palæolithic man and the stone weapons of the savages of historic times; as well as by discussing, with much care, the probable state of culture of these old British "Savages,"[1] as deduced by an

---

1 Again, we find a book which touches upon Machen's life-long interest in a Pre-Celtic race. Much later, in an essay entitled "A Midsummer Night's Dream" from the collection *Dog and Duck* (1924), Machen writes in detail about the excavation of Fairy raths, or mounds, in which are found the prehistoric living quarters of a vanished people.

examination of the intellectual development of the Esquimaux, Fuegians, Bushmen, &c., of our own time; and it is only by such comparisons and analogies that anything like a fair idea can be formed of a race about which we have such meagre knowledge. Mr. Allen Brown's book will be welcomed by all those who feel interested in this subject.

Sketches of Life in Japan.

August 1887, pp. 112

It would no doubt be possible for a traveller in Japan to bring back with him many valuable notes on the manners, customs, and antiquities of that strange country. This Major Knollys has not done; the student of folk-lore, anthropology, or philology will find nothing, or next to nothing, in these "Sketches" of which to make a note. But the book is nevertheless an amusing one. Everything is insignificant, but it is pleasantly set down. As the author seems to have but a slight knowledge of the Japanese language, his vocabulary beginning with "Ohaye" (meaning anything from "please do not fly into a passion" to "go to the deuce") and ending with "sayonara" (good-bye), we are not surprised that his information, except on superficial points, is decidedly limited. But we have very grave doubts whether it was worth Major Knollys's while to invest with the dignity of print such dialogue as the following. "'What is your religion, Kobe?' I ask my guide. 'Hum' (with the curled lip of derision), 'if I am anything at all, I am Shinto. But please make haste if you want to see yonder temple. Those lazy beasts' (with all the emphasis of hate) 'of priests are about to close the doors.'"

The First Nine Years of the Bank of England.

August 1887, pp. 112-113

The above volume professes to be an "inquiry into a weekly record of the price of Bank Stock from August 17, 1694, to September 17, 1703." It gives, in fact, a detailed and minute account of the Bank of England, when that great institution was a commercial enterprise, the success of which seemed very doubtful. The principal source of Professor Thorold Rogers's information is "Collections for Husbandry and Trade," published by one John Houghton, an apothecary, and a member of the Royal Society; and also "A Brief Relation of State Affairs," by Narcissus Luttrell, a work containing all the current information the writer could pick up between the years 1678 and 1714. But, besides fulfilling his immediate object of tracing the origin of the Bank, the writer gives, by the way, much curious information; for example, it is recorded that "in 1697 a 'good merchant's house,' close to the Royal Exchange, was offered at a rent of £60 a year . . . two houses were to be let in Fleet-street at £44 a year each; and an ale-house in the Strand, with three rooms on each floor, could be had for £20 to £30 a year."

The Brunswick Accession.

August 1887, pp. 113

This work gives the descent, from "Guelph, Prince of Scyrri" of the present reigning family of England; an account of the state of English politics in the first fourteen years of the eighteenth century; and the various intrigues on one side and the other which led to the Hanoverians obtaining the English crown. Mr. Thornton has done all this in a pleasant manner enough; but we do not quite see what want his book is intended to supply. Of late years the standard of historical composition has been greatly raised, and an author is expected to plead justification for a volume. This justification may be either new facts and discoveries, or else an original and striking method and point of view. We do not consider that "The Brunswick Accession" can plead either excuse for its appearance, and would counsel the author to devote his time and research to the less trite and trodden ways of history.

Arthur Machen

History of the Bassandyne Bible with Notices of the Early Printers of Edinburgh.

August 1887, pp. 113-114

This history of the first Bible printed in Scotland deserves to be read with great attention. The first two chapters, dealing with the Reformation in general, and the Scotch Reformation in particular, might, we think, have been condensed with advantage, but from the third chapter onwards all is valuable and noteworthy. The first printers in Scotland were Walter Chepman and Androw Myllar, to whom a patent was granted by James IV. in 1507. Until 1869 only two books could be attributed with any certainty to this early firm: the one a book of Ballads, and the other the "Breviarium Aberdonense." But in 1869 an "Expositio Sequentiarum" (1506) was discovered at Paris; and again in 1878 a work on Grammar was found in a private library at Dinant, in Brittany, both these works bearing Myllar's punning device—a windmill. For some time after these first-fruits of the press in Scotland there appears to have been a lull; the times were unsettled, the "New Light" of John Knox had to make way against considerable opposition. At any rate, it was not till 1568 that Robert Lekprevik, "our Soverane Lordis imprentare," received "license, priuelege, and power To imprent all and haill ane buke callit the Inglis bybill imprentit of before at Geneva." However, Robert Lekprevik fell into disgrace, and the work was undertaken by Thomas Bassandyne, a Scotchman, who had been educated at Antwerp, and had learnt the art of printing at Leyden—the "Lugd. Bat" of so many old title-pages. But Bassandyne himself had to "gang warily," the intolerant General Assembly being at the height of its power. This worthy court "declared and fund" that "Thomas Bassendie" had printit "ane baudy sang callit Welcome Fortune, at the end of ane Psalme Book," and required him to "delait" it. However, the Kirk was pacified, and in 1576 a licence was given to "Thomas Bassanden" and his partner, Alexander Arbuthnot, to "prent Bibillis in the vulgare Inglis toung." In July, 1579, the work was completed—and circulated—by the process of making the non-possession of "ane bybill" an offence against the law. Such, in brief, is the history of the "Bassandyne Bible" as told in the volume under consideration. Well written, well printed, and handsomely bound, as this book undoubtedly is, it is hard to understand how Mr. Dobson can have set such poor and common place woodcuts as "Burning Bibles at Paul's Cross," "The Chained Bible," and several others, beside the excellent facsimiles which are really worthy of a place in the work.

A Proposal for putting Reform to the Vote.

August 1887, pp. 114

This is a reproduction of Shelley's manuscript, introduced and commended to the faithful student of Shelley by Mr. Buxton Forman. Both the photo-lithography and the letterpress are admirably executed, and the editor, in his introduction, gives a well-drawn picture of those uneasy times, between 1815 and 1820, to which the pamphlet belonged. Shelley was then living at Albion House, Marlow, hence his designation on the title of the "Proposal." The pamphlet was published by Oilier in March, 1817, and attracted hardly any attention; it formed part of the heading to an article of Southey's in *The Quarterly Review*, but was not noticed in the text. Shelley's "Free List" is given in a brief appendix; copies were to be sent to the chief Reformers, such as Sir Francis Burdett, Mr. Brougham, Mr. Cobbett, &c.

The Allegorical Signification of the Tinctures in Heraldry.

September 1887, pp. 165-167

The student of Heraldry, who approaches the science rather from the literary and romantic than the purely antiquarian standpoint, will be dissatisfied in many ways with the modern text-books. Particularly, he will find either a cursory mention or no mention at all of the world of allegory in which the old heralds revelled. They saw everything in blazonry and blazonry in everything; the moral virtues, the stars, precious stones, trees, flowers, and birds, all were considered in relation to the tinctures of coat-armour. The following are in brief the principal significations of the metals and colours drawn from the famous pages of Guillim and Morgan:— [1]

1. *Or* is said to be composed of much White and a little Red, and of itself to betoken Wisdom, Riches, and Elevation of Mind: with *Gules* to spend his blood for the Wealth and Welfare of his Country: with *Azure* to be worthy of matters of Trust and Treasure: with *Sable* most rich and constant in everything, with an amorous mind: with *Vert* most joyful with the Riches of the World, and most glittering and splendid in youth. Of *precious Stones* it represents the Carbuncle or the Topaz: of the *Planets*, the Sun: of the *Elements*, Fire: of *human Constitutions*, the Sanguine: of *Trees*, the Cypress or Laurel: of *Flowers*, the Heliotropium: of *Fowls*, the Cock and Bird of Paradise: of *Beasts*, the Lion: and of *Fishes*, the Dolphin.

2. *Argent* signifies (*of worthy good Qualities*) Beauty and Gentleness of Behaviour: (*of the Planets*) the Moon: (*of the Elements*) the Water: (*of precious Stones*) the Pearl and Crystal: (*of Trees*) the Palm: (*of Flowers*) the Flower-de-Luce: (*of human Constitutions*) the Phlegmatic: (*of Beasts*) the Ermine, which is all white without any spot: (*of the Parts of a Man*) the brain, and (*of his Ages*) the old.

---

1 Antiquarian John Guillim (1565-1621) is best remembered for his foundational work *A Display of Heraldry* (1610). Likewise, Sylvanus Morgan (1620-1693) left a tome on the subject with the weighty title of *The Sphere of Gentry, deduced from the Principles of Nature: an Historical and Genealogical Work of Arms and Blazon, in Four Books* (1661). No doubt, Machen had read these works.

3. *Gules* is said to represent Fire, which is the chiefest, lightsomest, and clearest of the elements. Morgan says it denotes the Power of the Almighty: and of Virtues, Martial Prowess, Boldness, and Hardiness: with *Or* a Desire of Conquest, and with *Argent* a Depressing the Envious and Revenging the Innocent. Of spiritual Virtues *Gules* denotes Justice, Charity, and an ardent Love of God and our Neighbour: of worldly Virtues, Valour, Nobility, Hardiness and Magnanimity: of Vices, Cruelty, Choler, Murder, Slaughter: of the *Planets*, Mars: of *precious Stones*, the Ruby: of *Metals*, Copper: of *Trees*, the Cedar: of *Flowers*, the Piony, the Clove Gilliflower, and the Pink: of *Birds*, the Pelican: of the *Ages of Man*, the Manly: of the *Months of the Year*, March and July: of the *Days of the Week*, Tuesday.

4. *Azure*, says Guillim, consists of much Red and a little White, and represents the Colour of the Sky in a clear, sunshiny day. This colour signifies Justice, Chastity, Humility, Loyalty, and eternal Felicity: of worldly Virtues, Beauty, Praise, Meekness, Victory, Perseverance, Riches, Vigilance and Recreation: of the *Planets*, Venus and Jupiter: of *Metals*, Tin: of *precious Stones*, the Turquoise Stone: of the *Months of the Year*, September: of the *Days of the Week*, Wednesday and Friday: of Trees, the Poplar: of *Flowers*, the Violet: of *four-footed Animals*, the Chameleon: of *Fowls*, the Peacock: of *human Constitutions*, the Sanguine: and of the *Ages*, Youth.

5. A Green Colour is called *Vert*, in the Blazon of all under the degree of Noble; but in the coats of noblemen, it is called *Emerald*, and in those of kings, *Venus*. *Vert*, of Christian Virtues, denotes Charity and Hope, and among secular Virtues, Honour, Civility, and Courtesy: of the *Elements*, the Earth : of the *Planets*, Mercury: of *precious Stones*, the Emerald: of *Metals*, Quicksilver: of *Constitutions*, the Phlegmatic: of the *Ages of Man*, Youth: of the *Months of the Year*, April and May. Heralds say, likewise, that those who bear *Vert* in their coat-armour are obliged to support peasants and labourers, and particularly the poor that are oppressed. Sylvanus Morgan says:— "*Vert* with *Or* signifies Pleasure and Joy: and with *Argent* Innocent Love."

6. *Sable*, of the Virtues and Qualities of the Soul denotes Simplicity, Wisdom, Prudence, and Honesty: of the *Planets*, Saturn: of the *four Elements*, the Earth: of *Metals*, Lead, Iron: of *precious Stones*, the Diamond: of *Trees*, the Olive: of *Birds*, the Crow or Raven: of the *Ages of Man*, the last.

ARTHUR MACHEN

The Purpose of the Ages.

September 1887, pp. 171-173

Professor Sayce, in his preface to this book, declares its purpose to be the "putting of life into the dry bones and clothing them with flesh and beauty." In this object we think the authoress has, to a large extent, succeeded; and she is to be congratulated as one who has broken up new ground. The work is a poem in three books, its aim and end is to set forth what Mr. Shorthouse calls the Christian Mythos; to show it partly shadowed in and partly contending against the strange worships of Hittites, Babylonians, and Egyptians; and thus to lay open to the reader the vast store of knowledge which has of late years been recovered from mound, and tomb, and pyramid. It may be said at once that as a literary production "The Purpose of the Ages" is far from being satisfactory. The writer has a strange delight in the parenthesis, and this most clumsy and displeasing device appears on every page of the poem. The verse, too, is often rough and shapeless: and yet through it all there is an enthusiasm, a kind of heroic ring, which carries the reader on. But in the notes, which occupy more than 150 pages of the volume, historians and antiquaries will find much to interest them, and those who "want to know" about Hittites, Babylonian mythology, magic cylinders, the mysteries of the Egyptians, and the like abstruse objects of research, could not do better than consult this curious and original book. The poem opens with a description of the festival of "Sin or Hurki," the Moon-god of the Chaldeans, and the invocation of the god by the "Amil-Urgal," the priest appointed to watch for the rising of the Euphrates. "At the beginning of the month, at the rising of the night," chants the priest, "At the dawning of the second night of Nisan, Lo! the horns of great Sin they break through in the heavens, In the high heavens of Anu his horns pierce the gloom." A figure calls our attention to a note, and we learn or are reminded that Anu was the head of the Babylonian mythology, that his sign was a star and sometimes a Maltese cross. It is curious to find that "Mer," another deity mentioned, was styled "The Lord of Canals." Our readers will not be surprised to hear that he was a god of "a strong, positive character," and of somewhat pestilential attributes.

The next scene is "A Room in Terah's House," and we are given a minute account of the manner in which the young Abram broke the gods, his father's workmanship, placing the hammer in the hands of "Hurki." Abram, expelled by Terah, begins to wander over the earth in search of the true illumination, and we find him before long in the "Library of Agane," seeking wisdom from "Ismidagon, an old priest and astrologer." Respecting this early library some most curious information is given in a note, chiefly drawn from Professor Sayce's "Babylonian Literature." The library was founded by Sargon I., "perhaps one of the first of the Semitic conquerors who patronised literature; "at a period when Accad had become a learned language. The books were either translations of Accadian originals or based on Accadian texts. It is strange to think that the "bloom of Accadian poetry" was just 4,000 years ago, and strange to read of a library with classified catalogues (on clay) of books (also on clay) and regulations that "the reader is to write down the number of the tablet or book he requires and the librarian will give it him." So we pass to "A High-Place outside the walls of Sippara," and hear the song of the priests of the sun-god, at the sacrifice of the first-born son:—

"The head of the child for his own head,
   The brow of the child for his own brow,
   The breast of the child for his own breast."

The song of the priestesses of Ishtar, the words of Pharaoh's singer, "he who bare the books of Hermes," and all the mystic worship of Egypt follow us along this strange path among the tombs. "The Purpose of the Ages" is, as we have said before, a curious and valuable book, and we look for yet better things from the writer, when she has learnt that all literary work demands literary form; and that for the highest and most poetical of subjects the very best expression and style is requisite. It must be added that the arrangement of the notes is about as bad as it could be, and the student who desires to refer from the text to the notes will find he has to look first for the book, then for the division, in the text, and to repeat this process in the notes. We hope that in a second edition this defect may be remedied.

Hungary in Ancient, Mediæval, and Modern Times.

September 1887, pp. 173-174

This volume of the "Story of the Nations" series seems to us a little disappointing. A perfect history, we take it, should give as close a picture as the lapse of time renders possible of a nation; we should be able to say after reading such a book how people lived their every-day life; whereas this work is mainly an account of how they fought, revolted, and were suppressed by their rulers; how one king died violently and how another ruled his people with an iron rod. Of the manners, arts, and habits of the Hungarians in times past, we learn comparatively little; almost as little from the text as from the design on the cover, which depicts a lofty castle and an uncouth person smoking a long pipe. Of course it is well that all the sieges, gallant defences, battles, duels of kings, and sessions of great lords should be set down, but we should have liked to have seen a good deal more of the homely and common-place element in the book, and a little less of the heroic warfare and clash of swords. It need scarcely be said, however, that the reader will find much interesting matter in its pages; as, for instance, the description of the famous crown presented to Stephen, the first king of Hungary, by Pope Sylvester II. The crown of to-day, it appears, consists of two parts; the upper and more ancient, which adorned St. Stephen's head, and the lower and newer crown, which is stated to have been presented about 1073 by the Greek Emperor, Michael Ducas. The older crown is "formed by two intersecting hoops ... on its top is a small globe capped by a cross," beneath which is a picture of the Saviour, surrounded by the sun, the moon, and two trees; the surface of the two hoops is occupied by the figures of the twelve apostles. Curious also is the account of the early religion of the Magyars, who professed Shamanism. This system taught the adoration of one supreme being, styled Isten, and also the worship of the deities of the mountains, woods, thunder, springs, fire, &c. It seems to have been an eminently practical religion, if we may judge from a prayer in use among the Shaman worshippers of to-day:—

"O give us cattle, O God! Give food, O God! Give us a chief, O God!"

The Hungarians seem always to have been a tolerant people; and King Coloman (1095—1114) wisely declared in one of his edicts, "Of witches who do not exist at all no mention shall be made."

Arthur Machen

The Sieges of Pontefract Castle, 1644—1648.

September 1887, pp. 174-175

The editor of this book has with great care and patience collected a vast amount of information relating to the sieges which Pontefract Castle sustained during the Great Rebellion. The most important source from which the writer has drawn is "A Journal of the first Siege of Pontefract Castle, kept by Nathan Drake, a Gentleman Volunteer in it." A portion of the diary is given in fac-simile, by permission of F. H. Drake, Esq., a lineal descendant of the valiant volunteer. The first siege began on Christmas Day, 1644, and ended on July 19, 1645. Many a quaint, brave, and glorious deed is recorded in Mr. Drake's diurnal. Thus one morning "Came the beseegers with 50 musketeres, and lined the hedge and the dike with them; they playd very soare against the Castle but did no harme, onely a young maid was Drying of Clothes in Mr. Tayton's Orchard, She was shott into the head whereof she dyed that night." On another day a boy was dangerously shot "as he was getting of greene sawse." This, the editor explains, is a species of sorrel; we wonder whether the green sauce of Rabelais was of the same kind.[1] Both besiegers and besieged appear to have fought valiantly, but there could of course be only one result, since no succour or relief was able to reach the castle. But about three years after the Loyalists regained the castle, and the description of their enterprise is told in a letter published in 1702 by a printer in the Savoy. The writer was a Captain Paulden, who tells his correspondent that:—"In 1648, the first War being over, we that had served the King in it, submitting to our common Fate, lived quietly in the country, till we heard of an intended Invasion by Duke Hamilton; then we met frequently, and resolved to attempt the Surprising this Castle." With great daring the Royalists carried out their enterprise, and on the 3rd of June, 1648, took possession of the Castle and held it till after the King's death, proclaiming from

---

1 This reference can be found in Pantagruel, Chapter XXXI: "How Pantagruel entered into the city of the Amaurots, and how Panurge married King Anarchus to an old lantern-carrying hag, and made him a crier of green sauce."

it King Charles II. This book with its excellent commentary, index, plans, portraits, and reproductions, is really an excellent example of what such a work should be; but we think it deserved better type and better paper. We should advise the author, if he publish (as we hope he will) more collections on the history of Pontefract, to write his comment continuously, and not to break it up into short paragraphs, separated by rules.

Arthur Machen

Memoir of the Family of M'Combie.

September 1887, pp. 175

We cannot agree with the opinion expressed by the author in his preface, that much of what is contained in the work is not already known to probable readers. It seems to us that seventeenth century life in Scotland is one of the most familiar and trite of subjects; and in this "Memoir" there seems to be little that is really new or valuable. It will doubtless prove capital reading to the "Family of M'Combie," but to the general reader the histories of small Highland clans, how the M'Combie settled in Glenshee, and intermarried with Farquharsons, and how a heritable bond of manrent was granted to Lachlan Mor, the sixteenth chief of the M'Intoshes, &c., &c., seem somewhat wearisome and unprofitable.

Histoire de la Poésie Liturgique au Moyen Age. Les Tropes.

October 1887, pp. 241-243

Not many amongst our readers, we venture to say, except professed antiquarians, know anything about *tropes*, unless it is in the sense of *figures of speech*. What other meaning, then, can be applied to the word *trope*? M. Léon Gautier will give us at once a clear and correct answer. "Let us suppose ourselves, if you please, on that beautiful and radiant Christmas day, and listen to the *introit* of the Mass such as it was sung previous to the appearance of *tropes*; and as it is sung to-day in that Roman liturgy which has so fortunately been preserved from many dangerous innovations. 'Puer natus est nobis, et filius datus est nobis, cujus imperium super humerum ejus, et vocabitur nomen ejus magni consilii angelus. Ps. Cantate Domino canticum novum, quia mirabilia fecit. Gloria Patri,' etc.[1] Now this is what the above *introit* had become after the invasion, after the triumph of the *tropes*:—'Gaudeamus hodie quia Deus descendit de cælis, et propter nos in terris *Puer natus est nobis*, quem prophets diu vaticinati sunt. *Et filius datus est nobis.* Hunc a Patre jam novimus advenisse in mundum *cujus imperium super humerum ejus*, potestas et regnum in manu ejus. *Et vocabitur nomen ejus* admirabilis, consiliarius, Deus fortis, princeps pacis, *magni consilii angelus*. Ps. *Cantate Domino canticum novum, quia mirabilia fecit.* Gloria Patri,' etc. A *trope* is the interpolation of a liturgical text—interpolation which can be noticed from the ninth century to the twelfth in certain chant-books used by the churches of Germany, Italy, and France. It is the intercalation of a new text, devoid of authority, in an authentic and official sense." When M. Gautier speaks of texts *devoid of authority*, he means *liturgical* authority, not admitted in the service prepared by St. Gregory the Great. It is the history of these tropes that he gives in the present volume; and although he finds fault with them as intruders, he acknowledges that they did much for the progress of sacred music (they were all chanted)

---

1 Already in his late-twenties, Machen displayed a remarkable knowledge of liturgiology and no doubt this book added to it. The Roman Christmas Preface would return as a narrative device in a later story, *The Gift of Tongues* (1927), which is set in the 1880s.

by obliging their authors to compose long and carefully constructed melodies. A somewhat astonishing fact, says M. Gautier, is connected with the *tropes*:—"Transformed during the twelfth century into rhymed songs, they may be considered by the *savants* who make a point of referring to original texts as the source of all the Latin songs composed by the *Goliardi* of the twelfth and thirteenth centuries, whose satirical strains, alas! were directed against all holy things, especially the clergy, especially the Pope. These Goliardi began by singing *tropes* innocently, they soon proceeded to sing *gauloiseries*, and worse still. But that is not the greatest interest connected with this chapter of our literary history; and we must see in the *tropes* one of the origins of the modern drama. I did not say 'the origin,' and yet I am tempted to believe it. Through a series of transitions . . . the *tropes*, by degrees, have become *mysteries*, by degrees, again, the *mysteries* have become *plays (jeux)*, and finally the plays have developed into dramas written in the vernacular language."

We have thus given a summary of M. Gautier's first volume. Well known as Professor at the Paris Ecole des Chartes, and as one of the most distinguished mediæval scholars of the day, no one was better qualified to discuss about problems connected with the Romish liturgy, and the work we are now noticing will hold a conspicuous place near the editions of the "Chanson de Roland," the "Epopées Françaises," and the splendid volume on Chivalry. The history of Notkarius and of the monastery of Saint Gall enjoys an important share in this disquisition; for, as M. Gautier remarks, it is from Saint Gall that the *tropes* started on their journey through Western Europe. Three opinions as to their origin have been put forth and maintained with more or less success. That the first ones can be traced back earlier than the ninth century, that they were composed at Rome by Saint Gregory and his immediate continuators, is a thesis which no authentic document supports, and which has long since been abandoned. Some critics have named the year 1000 as the extreme date, and M. Gautier began by holding that opinion himself; but at that time he had examined only the Paris *tropaires*. At present, having studied the Saint Gall MSS., he has altered his views, and adopted the commencement of the tenth century as the starting-point. The derivation of the substantive *trope* is worth knowing. After giving us the various synonyms employed to designate chants and chanting during the Middle Ages, M. Gautier goes on:— "The word τρόπος has long passed into the Latin language. It was a musical term—

an exclusively musical one—meaning *mode*, and it soon assumed the signification of *melody*, by a transition which it is not difficult to understand. '*Tropus*,' says Forcellini, '*id est cantus, sonus*,' and it is in this sense that Fortunatus has frequently employed it: 'Reddebantque suos parvula saxa tropos.' 'Vox erat una tropis . . . mulceat atque aures fistula blanda tropos.' For us, therefore, *tropus* is and remains, even in the language of liturgy, a primitively musical expression, and which is originally the synonym of *melodiæ, cantilenæ, or of moduli, cantus rhythmici*. Martin Gerbert is right when he says:—'Tropi proprie sunt moduli, nomenque retinuerunt, cum illis verba sunt substituta, ut postea de sequentiis dicemus.'" The only mistake our author finds in this passage is the word *substituta*, instead of which he proposes *conjuncta*. M. Gautier's work is to be completed by the publication of a second volume. It may be considered as exhaustive on the subject of which it treats. It gives a description of the various *tropes* used in the Roman Catholic Church, and of the principal MSS. containing them; it is beautifully printed, and copiously illustrated with facsimiles of illuminations, ornamental letters, and music.

Arthur Machen

Shropshire Folk-Lore: A Sheaf of Gleanings.

October 1887, pp. 243-245

This third part of the Shropshire Folk-Lore commences with the joyous observances, songs, and rites of the harvest. With the Salopians there is no "kern-baby" or "mell-doll" carried home in triumph after the harvest done; but in place thereof a group of about twenty ears of corn left standing and knotted in the midst of the field. The men standing at a short distance cast their sickles at it, and whoever cut off the neck was reckoned the best man, and carried it home in triumph to the master's wife, who kept the "Gonder's neck," as it was called, till the next harvest. Another curious ceremony was that of crying the mare, a pretended offer of the "owd mar" to a farmer whose crops were still standing. The great aim of the harvesters was to "lug" (carry) all the corn without overthrowing a load; for the penalty for overthrowing was to "lose the guse" at the harvest-home supper. But if all had been safely brought in, the head man would stand up at the close of he feast and sing

"Well ploughed, well sown!
Well reaped, well mown!
Never a load o'erthrown!
Why shoudna we sing
Chorus: Harvest Home?"

In Shropshire traces of the rites of All Souls' Day still survive, and in many places poor children, and sometimes men, go out "souling," that is, they go round the neighbours' houses singing the ditty proper to the day and expecting a dole of food and money. Formerly, at all the "better-most houses," "soul cakes," buns made of light dough, spiced and sweetened, were given to the souling-children, but this custom seems to be almost obsolete. Many persons are still living in Shropshire who remember seeing at Christmastide a great trunk of seasoned oak, holly, yew, or crab-tree drawn by horses to the farmhouse door, and thence placed at the back of the wide hearth. Then the Christmas ale was tapped, and a great pewter tankard of drink served out to the log-bearers, who sang a Christmas carol by way of acknowledgment. For twelve days no ploughing nor spinning might be done, the distaff was dressed with flowers, and all days, except one, were fortunate. The exception was Innocents' Day, or Cross Day, on which it was unlucky to begin any undertaking. An interesting chapter is that on well-worship—a cult of the most primitive kind, which survives to the present day.[1] The most famous of the Shropshire wells is St. Oswald's Well, just outside Oswestry (Oswaldestre, in Welsh Croes Oswallt, the "tree," or stake, on which the body of the martyr was hung). From the pilgrimages to the well it is probable that the town of Oswestry took its origin. Near St. Oswald's Well is Woolston's Well, said to be dedicated to St. Winifred; and here the writer of Shropshire Folk-Lore saw in June, 1885, a broken arm in course of treatment, the injured man coming early every morning to dip the limb in the water. It is pleasant, in a way, to know that the old "wakes" are still observed in Shropshire, though with maimed mirth and degenerate observances. In 1868, at All Stretton Wake, the time-honoured custom of grinning through a horse-collar was performed, as also a smoking match, the prize to the man who could smoke half an ounce of tobacco in a "Broseley Churchwarden" in the shortest time. Many wakes had their peculiar delicates, "fig-cakes" and "mint-cakes" for instance. Then there were "furmety wakes," "cherry wakes," "eel-pie wakes," and "crab-wakes," the crabs being used not for eating but pelting.

1 Holy wells are found across the British Isles and throughout Machen's work. Most beautifully, a well dedicated to the mysterious St. Ilar figures prominently in the spiritual experiences of Ambrose Meyrick, the protagonist from *The Secret Glory* (1922).

Herefordshire Words and Phrases.

November 1887, pp. 303-304

The compiler of this excellent word-book has been told, it seems, that the work comes forty years too late, i.e., that in the past forty years the great bulk of the quaint words and phrases of the country folk of Herefordshire have gone out of use and memory. However that may be, Prebendary Havergal has contrived to collect about 1,300 words which are still current, and, in doing so, has discharged, we think, a most useful task. Some of the words have no apparent connection with or resemblance to their modern equivalents; for instance, "logger," a wedding-ring; "jubbin," a donkey; "tansilooning," beating; "torrel," a simpleton; "lattage," hesitation in speech; while other words are evident corruptions of ordinary English. The compiler gives the variants of bronchitis; they are "brontitis" (general form), "brownkites" (not uncommon), and "browntitus" (once heard). Then there are elaborate modern words used in a more or less perverted manner, as "avoirdupoised," which means in the district of Eardisland or "Yersland," to be in doubt about doing a thing; and "argufy," used in the sense of signify. Into another class fall the words which retain their old meaning, such as "impudence," indecency; and "consate," to fancy or imagine. Where, we wonder, could the Herefordshire peasant have found the word "tussiky," dry and hacking, as applied to a cough? Its connection with the Latin "tussis" is obvious, but the English rustic is far from familiar with the learned languages. Or why should the farmer occasionally call his horses by such strange names as "Venter" and "Queen Anne"? The collection of miscellaneous sayings and of Superstitions and Customs has only one fault—there is not nearly enough of it. We have space for one anecdote only, which runs as follows: "An old man used to come to the savings bank at Hereford who, when asked where he came from, in winter would reply, 'from Orcop, God help'; but, in the summer, his reply would be, "from Orcop, the Lord be praaysed.""

Chronicles of An Old Inn;
or, A Few Words about Gray's Inn.

November 1887, pp. 304

Readers of this work will find some information in it which might fairly come under the title, "Chronicles of an Old Inn." But the sub-title, alas! is by far the more appropriate. We have here "a few words about Gray's Inn," and a great many words about Smithfield martyrs, the noise of Holborn, the habits of the rooks in the precincts, the author's views on education, the character of Queen Elizabeth, and various other matters which have but small relation to Gray's Inn or the chronicles thereof. Indeed, the writer appends to one of his chapters a footnote to the effect that those who are interested in the history and customs of this old Inn are referred—to another book. This is as much as to say that the interested persons aforesaid will not have their curiosity gratified in Mr. Hope's volume, and this, in fact, is the case.[1]

1 One of the four traditional Inns of Court, Gray's Inn is an association for lawyers in London and holds a significant position in the city as a cultural and historical institution. For a time in the late 1890's Machen lived on Gray's Inn Road, so he knew the area quite well. Throughout his fiction, Machen uses Gray's Inn and the Road as landmarks in the adventures of his characters. In 1938, he sold a pleasant essay entitled "Gray's Inn Coffee House" to *Wine and Food* magazine which has been reprinted several times afterward.

Arthur Machen

The Parish Registers of Kirkburton, co. York.

November 1887, pp. 305

In the manner of Dr. Johnson,[1] we would say of this volume of Registers that its immensity wearies the imagination. The compiler must indeed be a very "painful" person to have transcribed about 11,000 entries of births, marriages, and deaths, and the service rendered to genealogists and Yorkshire antiquarians will, no doubt, be proportionate to her labour. The first entry is in 1541, and the last in 1654, so that a considerable amount of work still remains to be done. A note to one of the entries may, perhaps, tend to dispel some of the nonsense that is so often talked about "liberty of conscience" being enjoyed under the so-called Commonwealth. It is as follows:— "In 1651 Thomas Ellis, Thomas Roberts, and Richard Batty were imprisoned for holding the faith of the Society of Friends." There is an index (24 pp.) to all the names in the book.

1 Samuel Johnson (1709-1784) is often considered among the most distinguished writers in English literature. Throughout his work, Machen demonstrates a respect and affection for Johnson. As an actor, Machen performed as Dr. Johnson in an unreleased silent film, of which little is known and which is probably lost.

Epitaphs; or, Churchyard Gleanings

November 1887, pp. 305

The majority of the epitaphs contained in this compilation are well adapted for the "miscellaneous" column of a country paper, and we would suggest that in future editions the matter should be printed on one side of the paper only, so as to offer facilities to the exercise of the sub-editorial scissors. But a very small proportion of the whole collection can lay claim to devotion, wit, or quaintness of any sort, most being doggerel verses of an altogether hopeless description. After all, the only way in which epitaphs can be read to advantage is on their original stones beneath the old yew trees or on the ancient walls. Even the best seem to lose their savour of quaintness when they coldly stand in type, and this book, as we have said, is made up chiefly of the worst.

Arthur Machen

The Saracens from the Earliest Times to the Fall of Bagdad.

November 1887, pp. 305-306

This volume (one of the "Story of the Nations" series) is an excellent handbook for those who wish to trace the rise of, and progress made by, Islam. It does not pretend to any special originality of research or method; but it may be nevertheless commended to students, as giving the early history of Mohammedanism in a brief compass, and with great clearness. We should have liked Mr. Gilman to have expatiated at a little greater length on the early religion of the Arabs, and on the marvels of "Jinnistan," or Fairyland; but he has been obliged to condense his matter, and to keep strictly to the path of history. It is sad to find one's early conception of the good Caliph (or Kalif, as Mr. Gilman calls him) Harun-al-Rashid shattered beyond repair. Harun appears to have been a cruel and merciless tyrant; and his habit of walking in disguise about the streets of his city was apparently prompted by no creditable motives. There are excellent maps and illustrations to the work, and, best of all, a full index to the names, places, and subjects.

The Gnostics and their Remains,
Ancient and Mediæval.

November 1887, pp. 308-310

To many classes of students this, the second edition of "The Gnostics" will be in the highest degree welcome. For many years the first impression has been out of print, and has commanded a high price, so that a second and revised edition was really desirable. It need hardly be said that in this volume the antiquarian, the theologian, and the student of occult science, will find matter of the greatest interest. The writer begins by investigating the various origins of Gnostic theosophy, for the founders of the numerous systems of Gnosticism seem to have been men of excessively "broad" views, ready to gather an article of faith from the Christians, a bit of ritual from the worshippers of Mithras, an esoteric doctrine from the Buddhists, a theory from the Zoroastrians, an idea from the Platonists, and scraps of theurgy and magic from all sides and quarters. Hence the bewildering character of their systems (if they can claim such a title), and the great difficulty in unravelling the perplexed threads, some of which are pure Kabbalism, while others own Plato and Aristotle as their fathers. Egypt, too, is an important factor; so one cannot feel surprised at the remark of a scholar (quoted by Mr. King) that "the Gnostic theories reminded him of the visions that float through the brain of a madman." One of the author's most valuable authorities is the Gnostic treatise or Gospel, "Pistis Sophia," ascribed to the heresiarch Valentinus, and discovered by Schwartze in a Coptic MS in the British Museum. It professes to teach the "esoteric doctrine" of Christ given during the eleven years He passed on earth when He had returned from heaven after His Ascension. The whole is an extraordinary mixture of Kabbalism, Magism, and Christianity, and relates the triumphant passage of Christ and the Power Pistis-Sophia, who has been precipitated into the Abyss, and is borne up by Christ through the Twelve Æons. Mr. King next takes the various leaders or ignes fatui of Gnosticism, and gives an excellent account of the life and bewildering doctrines of Simon Magus, Manes, and Basilides. Then we have the teaching of the Ophites, or Naaseni, so-called from the Hebrew Nachash, "serpent." The chief object of their worship was the Agathodæmon or Chnuphis Serpent, depicted as having the head of a lion surrounded by a crown of seven or twelve rays. By an ingenious application of the analogy, "For as Moses lifted up the serpent in the wilderness, even so must the Son of man be lifted up," the Chnuphis Serpent became Christ. It was also, it appears, an excellent remedy for pleurisy when engraven on blue jasper and worn about the body, and, according to Mr. King, survives to this day, as a symbol of knighthood, in the collar of SS. Mithraism and the rites of Serapis are next compared with their Gnostic parallels, and the relation between Gnosticism and the superstition of the Evil Eye is traced. The remaining sections of this wonderful work treat of Abraxas gems, the various monuments of Gnosticism, and that much-debated question whether the Templars, Rosicrucians, and Freemasons draw their origins from these strange heretics of the second century. Into this tangled maze of occultism and obscurity we cannot enter; but to all who would do so Mr. King will be the best and the most reliable of guides. The book is illustrated with numerous woodcuts and thirteen plates of gems, talismans, and mystic marks; and many of the so-called Gnostic gems, it may be remarked, are nothing more than amulets against disease, invented and cut by mediæval quacks. There is an excellent index and a bibliography to this strange record of theories, which at their best are (as St. Augustine declares) but "splendid phantoms," and at their worst the sick fancies of disordered minds.

Vos Valete et Plaudite.

November 1887, pp. 320

With this November Number the Editor of *Walford's Antiquarian* has to bid his readers farewell. Twelve volumes of the Magazine have now been issued; and it is hoped that in each and all of these students of the old days have found, and will continue to find, "somewhat saved and recovered from the deluge of time." We have endeavoured not only to set before our readers the remains and memorials of the past, but also to note down the changes, whether of true restoration or of wanton destruction, that our own age is working. In our pages are the records of forgotten lives and neglected books brought once more to light, of old customs and usages that had faded almost out of recollection, and of those vestiges and shadows of the former time that still linger in the by-ways of the nineteenth century. It might safely, then, be said that such a work as this could not be unprofitable; but our readers will remember the words of George Herbert:—

"Sweet spring, full of sweet days and roses,
A box where sweets compacted lie,
My music shows ye have your closes,
    And all must die."

So after this November the Magazine will itself be numbered among the "portions and parcels of the past," leaving behind it, we trust, no ungracious memory. And thus, like the Cantor at the end of a Roman comedy, we say, "Farewell, and give your applause!"

WELSH PLACE-NAMES.—Many Welsh place-names give unmistakeable evidence of the Roman occupation; thus Pont-Sadarn, near Caerleon-on-Usk, is, of course, *"Pons Saturni"*; while Clemendy, a farmhouse in the same district, is a hybrid word, probably composed of *"colomen"* (Lat. *columba*) and ty, a house. Ystrad, a common prefix in place-names, is the Latin stratum, and -allt, -ffin, and -eglwys are very evidently descendants of *altus, finis,* and *ecclesia.* In the purely native place-names a description of the situation is mostly contained, sometimes of a rather poetical kind; thus Nant-yr-eos, "Nightingale's Brook," Twyn-yr-haul (Greek ἥλιος), "Sunny Hill," Llwyd-coed, "Grey Wood" Pantêg, "Fair Valley," and so forth. From a bend in a river or brook comes Kemeys (*cam,* crooked, and *wy,* water); to a rapid mountain stream the name Torfan (stone rolling) is given, though since the setting up of iron-works along the banks this name has been almost superseded by that of Avon Llywd, "Grey Water." Croes, a cross, often occurs; Waun-yr-croes, the meadow of the cross; Croeswen, the white cross, are examples. Cefn-vynach (by mutation from mynach) the "Monks' Ridge," is the name of an old mansion, formerly the grange of an abbey. The names of Welsh saints enter into the formation of many words, the patron saint, David, appearing in his native dress as Dewi in Llanddewi (llan, answering in meaning to the Greek τέμευος, is considered by Prof. Morris to be akin to *lawn*). St. German, the French Bishop who routed Pelagius, gives his name to several parishes called Llanarmon, while the very common Llanfihangel testifies to the popularity of St. Michael the Archangel in the Welsh Church of the Middle Ages;

the Blessed Virgin Mary (also a favourite saint) may be discovered in Llanfair, and St. Patrick (vulgarly considered to be an Irishman) in Llanbadrig.[1]

PRINTERS' ERRORS.—When the unabridged edition of Webster's Dictionary first appeared, that great scholar, Caleb Gushing, wrote a criticism on the stupendous work, saying that, for its size, it had as few errors as could be expected. This puzzled the editors, who asked an explanation of Mr. Cushing's information on the subject of those errors. In reply Mr. Gushing marked 5,000 mistakes in the volume which had been presented to him and sent it back. There is, probably, no book in existence that is absolutely free from errors of the press.

EARLY PUBLISHING.—It is probable that the first printers did not take off more than two or three hundred, if so many, of their works; and therefore the earliest printed books must have been still dear, on account of the limited number of their readers. Caxton, as it appears by a passage in one of his books, was a cautious printer, and required something like an assurance that he should sell enough of any particular book to repay the cost of producing it. In his "Legend of Saints" he says, "I have submysed myself to translate into English the 'Legend of Saints' . . . and William, Earl of Arundel, desired me—and promised to take a reasonable quantity of them—and sent me a worshipful gentleman, promising that my said lord should during my life give and grant to me a yearly fee, that is to note a buck in summer and a doe in winter."

A LEGEND CONFIRMED.—The Dean of Winchester, in a letter to *The Hampshire Independent*, relates a curious circumstance in connection with the excavations going on in Winchester Cathedral

---

1 Many of the place-names listed above are to be found throughout Machen's writing. Some examples: 1) Machen's Rabelaisian romance *The Chronicles of Clemendy* would be published the following year; 2) The Healing Cup of Nant Eos is mentioned in *The Great Return* (1915) as part of a narrative anecdote reputedly taking place in 1887, the year of this article; 3) Also in *The Great Return*, we find Croeswen, the site of a miracle; 4) Kemeys is found in Clemendy, and mentioned in *Far Off Things* as inspirational for *The Great God Pan* and *The Inmost Light* (1894); 5) Machen grew up in the rectory of Llanddewi Fach; and 6) Llanfihangel is referenced in two novels–*The Hill of Dreams* (1907) and *The Terror* (1917).

churchyard: "The 'Gloucester Fragments,' an Anglo-Saxon life of St. Swithun, written towards the end of the tenth century, tell us that the solemnity of moving the good Saint's bones from the churchyard to St. Ethelwold's new church was heralded by a string of miracles and marvels. In one of these tales the Saint appeared to an aged smith, bidding him let Bishop Ethelwold know that it was time for the translation to take place. The smith demurred, and did not do it till after the Saint appeared to him thrice; then, thinking the matter serious, he went into the churchyard where the Saint's tomb was, and, taking hold of an iron ring securely fastened into the block of stone which formed the top of the coffin, he prayed that if he who had appeared to him lay buried there, the ring might come easily out of the stone. Then he gave a pull, and behold! it came out as easily as if it had been bedded in sand. He next stuck the staple of it back in the hole whence it had been drawn, and now it stuck so tight that no man could move it again. This is the legend; now for the curious coincidence. I had set the men to drive a trench due north from the north-west door of the church, because constant tradition has affirmed that just there, under the drip of the eaves of the roof, St. Swithun was buried by his own command. Our trench crossed the exact spot at which he was said to have lain till moved by St. Ethelwold; and there, at a depth of nine feet below the present surface, well beneath some interesting chalk cists containing bodies, which had certainly never been moved for many centuries, the men threw out an iron ring and staple attached. The ring is nearly four inches in diameter, the staple just five inches long. Though, through lying for ages in the damp earth, ring and staple are much corroded, still there cannot be the least doubt as to their character and original intention. It is just such a ring as the legend mentions. Have we found, then, a genuine relic of the Saint? He would be a bold man who should declare that we have; all I will venture to say is that the coincidence of its discovery with the Anglo-Saxon legend is very curious; and that everyone may think of it exactly as he will. Is it not delightful to live in a place where everything one comes across *si non è vero è ben trovato?*"

A RAMBLE IN LONDON.—In the midst of a small folio account-book that belonged to the Hebden family, yeomen of the parish of Barton-le-Street, Yorks, and which extends from 1662 to 1762, occurs an entertaining account of the sightseeing of James Hebden during a brief visit to the Metropolis in the middle of last century. It is headed "My Ramble in London," and extends over two pages. The following is a *literatim* copy of his first day's journey:—"On Wednesday ye 31 of October 1750. In ye Morning round St Pauls; after Breakfast down Ludgate; from thence to New Markit fleet Street past ye Temple through ye Barr where ye Rebbles Heads are: down ye Strand to Shering Cross St James's Square pelmell St James's House where we Saw ye guar ye releved and the guard room walked round ye Pallas into ye mell and ye Park at ye upper End of ye Mell is Buckinham house a very fine one; and at ye East End of ye Pallas is ye House of ye late Dutches of Maulbrough A finer House than ye Kings; from thence Up St James's Street where we Saw three of ye Kings Coaches and 2 Troops of Horse Guards going to meet ye King in his return from Hannover; from thence Cross pickadilley to Newport Markttt; Down long Acre Cross Drury lane down great Queen Street into Lincoln's Inn Square at ye Corner ye which is ye fine House of ye Duke of New Castles; from thence into Howborn to furnivals Inn; to Snow Hill past St Pulchers Church; through Newgate into Newgate Markitt; where we Dined at Mr Fann's; then after Dinner we went to see my Horse and Mr Heyams where we drank a pint of chirrey, from thence to Little Britain; down Cheap Side to ye royal Exchainge to ye Bank of England where we See ye great Treasure House of ye Nation; from thence Up Corn Hill; down Gratious Street to ye Monniment at ye foot of the Bridge; Down Terns Street to Billingsgate to Bare Key; to ye Custom House, and from thence to ye Tower; where I See 5 Lyons 2 Tygars one Lepord and other wild Creators; took Coach on tower Hill where ye Rebbell Lords were beheaded and Came back to Newgate Markitt in ye Evening all very merry."—*Reliquary.*[2]

THE "LEATHER BOTTLE" INN, COBHAM.—The "Leather Bottle" Inn, at Cobham, near Rochester, rendered famous by

---

2 Machen's love for rambling the vast wilderness of London forms a favorite theme of his autobiographical writings such as *The London Adventure* (1924). During the '80s, this pastime filled empty hours whilst feeding his fervent imagination, which in turn, unfolded into the distinct geography found in his horrors tales of the following decade. Of further note, the finding of a forgotten and curious travelogue of London contributes to the mystical adventures of characters found in Machen's final novel, *The Green Round* (1933) and a late story: *N* (1936).

Charles Dickens, was destroyed by fire early on the morning of Good Friday. Those familiar with the pages of "Pickwick" will remember that this pleasant country inn was chosen as a temporary residence by the heart-broken Mr. Tracy Tupman, after his desertion by the faithless Rachael Wardle, and it was there where Mr. Pickwick and his friends found him, not, as they were led to expect, in a state of extreme mental depression bordering on distraction, but seated at a table "well covered with a roast fowl, bacon, ale, and etceteras, and as unlike a man who had taken leave of the world as possible." Although the "Leather Bottle" had frequently changed hands since that time, it always preserved those characteristic features so happily described in "Pickwick," and thereby proved a constant attraction to visitors from all parts of the world, who went to pay homage to the genius of the great magician. There always remained "the long, low-roofed room, furnished with a number of high-backed, leather-cushioned chairs of fantastic shapes, and embellished with a great variety of old portraits and roughly coloured prints of some antiquity." It was at Cobham where Mr. Pickwick made his famous antiquarian discovery, of the stone bearing the strange inscription: "Bill Stumps his Mark."

MAZES.—Of the many species of mazes one of the most curious is the so-called "Journey to Jerusalem." This was the plan of a labyrinth, traced out on the pavement of a church in tiles of various colours; the centre of the maze representing both the actual and the symbolical city of Jerusalem. To track out the windings of one of these "journeys," was a penance often enjoined, the penitent kneeling all the while, and patiently following the various turnings and returnings till he reached the Jerusalem in the midst of the mizmaze. Along the way were pictured symbols of the perils, toils, and sorrows of the journey of this mortal life, so that in fact the penitent made a kind of "Pilgrim's Progress" in a brief compass. At the same time, allusion was doubtless made in these "journeys" to the crusades for the possession of the actual city; it was perhaps felt to be a kind of composition for staying at home instead of waging the War of the Cross in Palestine. Of these mazes (of which there were many in France) few now remain. Some were wantonly destroyed at the Revolution, some taken up by the authorities because of the noise made by children in tracing them out, and some "restored" out of existence for no reason in particular.

CURIOSITIES OF HYDROPHOBIA.—It is well known that Goldsmith states that the mad dog became mad to "serve his private ends;" this explanation, however, either had not occurred to, or at any rate was not accepted by the ancients. They said that to drink sea-foam caused rabies; while the Arab dogs to this day go mad when they "taste of flesh that falls from heaven." Another theory makes a worm, residing in the tail, the cause; hence the custom of biting off dogs' tails. The same diversity of opinion exists respecting the cure of hydrophobia. Pliny suggests either the placing the burnt cinder of a dog on the wound, or else to eat the flesh of a dog, boiled; while there is, of course, the proverbial recipe—a hair of the dog that has bitten one.

THE "MABINOGION."—According to Professor Rhys, the term "Mabinogion" applies, strictly speaking, only to four particular tales. These formed the stock-in-trade of literary apprentices, who had not yet learnt the art of versing, and who were licensed to go about repeating these four stories in question. But a larger group of tales was also called "Mabinogion" in a sort of indefinite way, and the latest of them are purely Arthurian. The purely Welsh tales, "Mabinogion," had, as their motive, mainly the machinery of magic or the supernatural. Then when the Normans conquered parts of South Wales, they got hold of the Welsh literature and assimilated it to suit their tastes, and it passed into English and Scottish hands, and even extended over the west of Europe, including Iceland. But the Normans gave it their own forms. Their machinery was knight-errantry and individual bravery. Then in time these non-Welsh versions—Norman, English, and Scottish—reacted on the purely Welsh one; in fact, some of the Arthurian tales were probably a good deal influenced by the reaction of the Norman versions and those based on them.

MONASTIC GARDENS.—The monks, after the conversion of the Anglo-Saxons to Christianity, appear to have been the only gardeners. As early as 674 we have a record, describing a pleasant and fruit-bearing close at Ely, then cultivated by Brithnoth, the first Abbot of that place. The ecclesiastics subsequently carried their cultivation of fruits as far as was compatible with the nature of the climate, and the horticultural knowledge of the Middle Ages. Whoever has seen an old abbey, where for generations destruction only has been at work, must have almost invariably found it situated in one of the choicest spots, both as to soil and aspect; and, if the hand of in judicious improvement has not swept it away, there is still the "Abbey-garden." Even though it has been wholly neglected—though its walls be in ruins, covered with stonecrop and wallflower, and its area produce but the rankest weeds—there are still the remains of the ancient fruit trees, the venerable pears, the delicate little apples, and the luscious black cherries. The chestnuts and the walnuts may have yielded to the axe, and the fig trees and vines died away; but sometimes the mulberry is left, and the strawberry and the raspberry struggle among the ruins. There is a moral lesson in these memorials of the monastic ages. The monks, with all their faults, were generally men of peace and study; and these monuments show that they were improving the world, while the warriors were spending their lives to spoil it. In many parts of Italy and France, which had lain in desolation and ruin from the time of the Goths, the monks restored the whole surface to fertility, and in Scotland and Ireland, there probably would not have been a fruit tree till the sixteenth century, if it had not been for their peaceful labours. It is generally supposed that the monastic orchards were in their greatest perfection from the twelfth to the fifteenth centuries.

AN OLD ENGLISH TOWN.—Half a century ago Morley would have presented a fine picture of a good old-fashioned Yorkshire village. Once a day the heavy red mail coach, with the royal arms painted on the door panel, rumbled through its principal street to or from Leeds, and a single copy of the Leeds weekly journal found its way to the village inn. Night work was then done by tallow candles; women wore panniers in place of pockets; knee breeches, leggings, and shoe buckles still adorned the men; salt was fourpence half penny a pound, white bread was a Sunday delicacy, and postage was elevenpence to London. A working man's cottage was a one-story house of two rooms, the walls of rough stones, the roof of thatch, with a single door held fast by a wooden latch, and a solitary window at the back of one "living room." Its chief articles of furniture were the oak dresser and the tall clock. Over the fireplace the mantelshelf served as a general hold all. Here stood the tinder box, the candle snuffers and tray, and perhaps some bits of Leeds pottery. Overhead hung herbs in process of drying for domestic use—"agrimony," "betony," "camomile," "eyebright," and the like. It was a simple and home like interior, whose type is now fast passing away even in England where the old lingers so long.

PROGRESS IN BOOK-BUYING.—After the "Colloquia" of Erasmus had gone through six editions, Simon de Collines published, in Paris, an edition of twenty-four thousand. He "sold out" in a few days, and his edition was so worn away by perpetual reading that copies of it are now very scarce. The "Colloquia" are in Latin, and (if this anecdote of Charles Nodier is correct) one can precisely estimate the advance in the love of reading which has been made in three hundred years. To be sure, we have, perhaps, no Erasmus among us at present; but, even if we had, would a thousand people buy his book in a year?

LAW AND ASTROLOGY.—A modern astrologer being "fined £5 and costs by the police magistrate for casting horoscopes, he appealed to the Queen's Bench Division, and his appeal was dismissed with contumely, Mr. Justice Denman declaring: 'It was too nonsensical to suppose for a moment that a man could really believe that he had the power to predict the fortune of another man by merely knowing the day on which he was born. We did not live in times in which it was possible to think that anybody could believe such nonsense, unless he was a lunatic, and there was in this case no evidence of insanity.' Seldom has a judge uttered a dictum more arrogant and more untrue. At this moment seven-eighths of the subjects of Her Majesty, including the great tributaries of the East, implicitly believe in astrology. The astrologer is an important functionary in the Courts of Constantinople, Teheran, and Pekin. Nay even in the United Kingdom, there are more who believe in astrology than most people imagine. Zadkiel is read by duchesses and Cabinet Ministers, but, owing to the overbearing arrogance of the unbelievers, they seldom confess their faith."—*Pall Mall Gazette.*

STONE IMPLEMENTS.—Dr. Anderson, in his "Bronze and Stone Ages," goes into interesting details as to the stone tools found in Scotland, which appear to have been generally discovered by accident while the land was being broken up, or the bogs reclaimed. There are two kinds of axes, perforate and imperforate, the imperforate being much the more common. They are wrought out of all sorts of material—granite, gneiss, porphyry, basalt, and sandstone. They vary greatly in size, but all have a shaft hole; some are sharpened and either single or double edged, while others have both the edges blunted. A great variety of stone hammers has been dug up, some of the specimens being elaborately decorated; while we are let into the secrets of their careful polishing by the occasional discovery of grinding stones which have seen no little service. Comparing the shapes of these axes of stone with those of our modern axes of iron, Dr. Anderson comes unhesitatingly to the conclusion that the one is as much a product of thought and culture as the other. With them, as with the weapons, "we find the workmanship of the best examples faultless, the polish perfect, and the edges as regular and finely drawn from the face of the instrument as it is possible to make it with the aid of machinery and scientific appliances."

A STRANGE BURIAL.—In the will (dated 1601) of Henry Seaman, a rich Cambridgeshire yeoman, the testator gives the following directions for his funeral:—"My body to be broughte to the earthe from whence yt came and to be buryed in the churche of Soham at my stooles end and there to be set downe righte up, standing vppon my feete in a cophine. And for my soule peale to be runge twelve howers I give for the ringing thereof tenne shillinges of money. And I give to the churche for breaking up the pauiment and to be set vp at my stooles end fyve and twentie shillinges of money. And allso I give vnto them that shall ringe at my Buriall daye and to ringe fyve dayes after to make up sixe dayes to be range for with my buryall daye; to be so runge for presentlie after my buryall, they to have for euery daye eighte shillings. And allso my will is that at my bringing to the churche to be buryed, that I have twoe minstrells to playe some musicke before me to the churche to be buryed, and to playe all the day after, and they to have for their laboure and paynes takinge seaven shillinges. And allso my will is that at my buryall daye my executrix shall make some good chere with her neighboures, and shall give to the poore people fortie shillinges . . . Within twoe yeres after my buryall my executrix shall give three poundes of money; that is to saye, thirity shillinges a yere towards the releife of the ympotent, lame and blynde."

IN AN OLD LIBRARY.—Sixtus IV. set on foot a plan for the reorganisation of the Vatican Library, which then contained 3,650 volumes. In 1475 Platina was made librarian, and a new epoch in the history of libraries began. Platina's account-book has lately been printed by M. Muntz, and hence the varied nature of the librarian's duties can be seen. He had to buy books, send out copyists, procure skins for binding, and, in fact, supervise every detail of a book's production as well as its use. The books were arranged in four rooms: the first, open to the public, contained Latin books; then came the Greek room; then the reserved books, perhaps distinguished by the richness of their binding; finally, the room in which were kept the Papal archives. Platina began a definite alphabetical catalogue for the use of readers, and also undertook the cataloguing of the archives. He further supervised the reading-room, in which the books were chained and open for the public use. The notice to readers smacks of the directness of Sixtus IV.:—"No one in the library is to talk loudly or contentiously, and persons moving from place to place must not climb over the benches or make a noise with the feet. All books must be closed and replaced in their proper places. Anyone transgressing these regulations will be ejected with disgrace, and forbidden access to the library in the future." Platina's accounts show that the reading-room was well warmed, and that the comfort of readers was carefully attended to. Moreover, books were lent at Platina's discretion to cardinals, scholars, and even to strangers passing through Rome. The register of books lent opens as follows:—"Whosoever thou art that writest thy name in this volume on account of books lent from the pontifical library, know that thou wilt incur the wrath and anathema of the Pope unless thou return them intact and presently. This warning Platyna, librarian to His Holiness, giveth to thee."

EPITAPH OF JOHN RUSKIN'S PARENTS.—In the little churchyard of Shirley, not far from the residence of the Archbishop of Canterbury, there is a ponderous gravestone, bearing the following characteristic inscriptions:—

Here rests, from day's well-sustained burden, John Thos. Ruskin, born in Edinburgh, May 10, 1785. He died in his home in London, March 3, 1854. He was an entirely honest merchant, and his memory is to all who keep it, dear and helpful. His son, whom he loved to the uttermost, and taught to speak truth, says this of him.

Here, beside my father's body, I have laid my mother's. Nor was dearer earth ever returned to earth, nor purer life recorded in heaven. She died December 5, 1861, aged 90.

CHIGWELL CHURCH, ESSEX.—This church, which is connected with scenes in "Barnaby Rudge," and otherwise historically interesting, has lately been reopened, after restoration. It is noteworthy as the burial-place of Archbishop Harsnett, a native of Colchester, who, in a somewhat weak moment, left the town of his birth his important library. His epitaph, preserved at Chigwell Church, and written by himself, runs as follows:—"Here lies Samuel Harsnett, formerly Vicar of this Church, and afterwards, first the unworthy Bishop of Chichester, then the more unworthy Bishop of Norwich, and lastly the very unworthy Archbishop of York." Archbishop Harsnett was instituted Vicar of Chigwell in 1597, being then 36 years of age.

A COCK-MATCH.—"To be fought at the Red-House in Cardiff, between Vaughan Lloyd, of Taneralth, and Roger Powell, of Energlynn, Esqrs. to produce 41 Cocks on each Side in the Main, for 10 Guineas a Battle and 200 the odd Battle, and 20 in the Bye's for four Guineas a Battle. To weigh on Monday the 28th Day of May, and fight the four following Days. N. B. Whereas Ralph Bowen of the Red-House has been at the whole Expence in building a compleat new Set of Pens and Pit, he humbly hopes that all Noblemen and Gentlemen that design to partake of the Sport will be so good as to put up at his House, where they may depend upon the best of entertainment.—*Advertisement of 1750.*

CINDERELLA'S SLIPPER.—An argument has arisen whether Cinderella's slipper was of glass (*verre*), or of fur (*vair*). The British Museum Library does not possess the original edition of the story of Cinderella, and perhaps the only copy known in England was that of the Duke of Hamilton. This had belonged to Charles Nodier, and was sold at his sale for 112 francs—less than £5, at the Hamilton Sale (1884); it was purchased by Mr. Quaritch for £85. The copy was a fine one, bound by Bauzonnet in blue morocco, though described as lacking the list of errata. A copy of this edition, then, the Museum has not, nor has it the Holland edition of 1697. But the Museum has a copy of a Dutch edition of 1698. This, however, is not easy to find in the catalogue, because it is attributed to Perrault d'Armancour—"le fils de Monsieur Perrault de l'Academic François," says the title-page, making one error in spelling and one in grammar—and not to Charles Perrault. In this copy the slipper (*pentoufle* it is called) is certainly of *verre* not *vair* and the reading is borne out by the illustration.

MUM.—This mysterious beverage, which is still included in Acts of Parliament relating to brewing, seems to have been composed of extraordinary and heterogeneous materials. The "first matter" was water, to which were added wheat-malt, oat-malt, and ground beans. Then the brewer of mum gives reins to his Gothic imagination, and begins to cast in, with a kind of romantic frenzy, the inner rind of the fir, the tops of the fir and birch, *carduus benedictus*, flowers of rosa solis, burnet, betony, marjoram, wild thyme, and other herbs better known by students of middle English than gardeners. After this eccentric mixture has duly worked, the brewer puts into the cask ten new-laid eggs, the shells not being cracked or broken, and with this crowning absurdity he "stops all close," and sits down to wait for two years, at the end of which period the strange liquid is said to be drinkable.

AN OLD CALENDAR.—Amongst some Roman antiquities recently discovered at Grand, in the Vosges, was a brass disc, exactly a Roman foot in diameter, which had evidently been used as a calendar. Close to the edge it presents a number of small holes, each of which corresponds with each day in the year. Opposite some of those holes are inscriptions indicating the eighth day of the kalends, the nones and the ides of each month. The names of forty-eight days in the year were thus inscribed on the disc, and the names of those corresponding with the blank holes on the disc could be easily supplied. The chief object of that instrument was to indicate the length of the day at each season. A mark is made on the disc between the centre and the circumference opposite the winter months. That mark is so placed that its distance to the holes corresponding with the various days is proportionate to the length of those days and in indirect ratio with the length of nights during the same period of the year. Amongst the Romans, the exact knowledge of the length of days was indispensable for controlling time as indicated by *clepsydræ*.[3] Indeed, the Romans used to reckon twelve hours in every season

---

3 "Clepsydræ" is a type of clock depending upon the flow of water or mercury through a small aperture to measure time.

from sunrise to sunset, the only difference being that the length of the hour varied according to the season. The calendar found at Grand seems to have been made for the latitude of Rome.

CAXTONIANA.—A copy of the first edition of Caxton's "The Game and Playe of Chesse," black letter, "Ffynysshide of the last day of Marche the yer of our Lorde Gode. a. thousande foure hundrede ande lxxiiii," was sold by Messrs. Puttick & Simpson in December last for £645. This is the first book to which Caxton put a date. The following is the auctioneer's description:—"A perfect copy (except the 2 blank ll.). Of extraordinary rarity. This copy was unknown to Mr. Blades, who enumerates only four other perfect copies; the one in the King's Library in the British Museum being slightly shorter than the present. This copy is on stout paper, very sound and genuine throughout, though slightly stained, and having an erasure of four words on the 21st and 22nd lines of the 51st leaf. It measures 10 1/8 x 7 1/8 in., and is bound in old calf of the early part of the seventeenth century."

PALMISTRY.—There is an unrepealed Act of Parliament against the practice of Palmistry, which runs as follows:—"And all proctors and pardoners going about without sufficient authority, and all other idle persons going about or abiding in any city and practising palmistry, shall, if found guilty, before two justices of the peace, be punished by whipping two days together. And if he eftsoons be guilty of a same or like offence, then he is to be scourged two days, and the third day put upon the pillory from 9 till 11 o'clock in the forenoon, and have one of his ears cut off, and if he offend a third time he is to have a like punishment of whipping and the pillory, and then his other ear cut off."

THE ARCHBISHOP'S PALACE AT CROYDON.—An interesting gathering was recently held at the Archbishop's Palace, Croydon, the Mayor, some members of the Town Council, and several fellows and members of the Archæological and Antiquarian Societies of London and of Surrey being present. Mr. E. Loftus Brock, F.S.A., acted as cicerone to the company, whom he guided over the hall, the chapel, the (so-called) guard-room, the music gallery, the long gallery, Queen Elizabeth's bedchamber, and the other parts of the building which are still standing. The visitors afterwards assembled in the chapel, where Mr. Brock read a paper on the architecture and the historical associations of the structure. Mr. Brock showed that the chapel, which is of Tudor date, stands on the site and foundations of an earlier building. The great hall is of considerably older date, and shows the armorial bearings of Archbishop Stafford, who erected it, on its walls and the corbels which support the timber of its fine open roof. The entrance to this hall, at its north-eastern angle, is more than half a century older. In this hall Queen Elizabeth must often have sat as a Royal guest, and so probably did James I. of Scotland, who spent some years as a prisoner here in the time of Archbishop Courtenay, and Queen Mary once at least held her Council here with Cardinal Pole at her side. Queen Elizabeth's bedchamber still remains substantially the same as three centuries ago, though its panelling and its ornamental ceiling have disappeared. The long gallery, which runs along the entire southern side, the exterior walls of which were cased in red brick by Archbishop Wake, is of special interest as being the place in which Queen Elizabeth is said in history to have bestowed the Great Seal of the Lord Chancellor on the handsome Sir Christopher Hatton in 1587, just three centuries ago; and it is very little altered since that day, though partitioned off in order to make modern bedrooms.

"YANKEE" AND THE "STARS AND STRIPES."—When the Pilgrim Fathers landed on Plymouth Rock, the friendly Indians asked of what people they were, to which query they replied "English." But the red man could not twist his tongue around that word, and "Yangeese" was as near as he could get to it. It was but a very short time, and by a natural and easy transition, before "Yangeese" became transformed into "Yankees." Sulgrave, "the ancestral home of the Washington family, from whom sprang the renowned George Washington, first President of the United States, lies about three miles to the south-west of Morton Pinkney, in a secluded valley on the left-hand side of the road leading to Banbury. Just outside the village, standing about two fields back from the road, is the ancient manor-house erected by Laurence Washington about the year 1560, still bearing on the spandrils of the outer porch his coat of arms, the 'Stars and Stripes,' inscribed on a shield, with his crest, a raven, above it." Thus both the distinctive names by which Americans are known, and the banner of their nation may be traced to sources purely English.

THE EARLY CUSTODY OF DOMESDAY BOOK.—Three theories have been entertained by modern scholars upon the early custody of Domesday Book:—(1) The "Winchester" theory, or that in favour of the preservation of Domesday in the Winchester treasury from 1086 to an indefinite date not earlier than the close of the twelfth century, or even later. (2) The "Westminster" theory, depending on the statements of Ingulphus and of the Burton and Bermondsey chroniclers. This theory is in effect that the book was preserved continuously at Westminster. (3) The "Winchester-Westminster" theory, which insists on its removal from the former to the latter place at a comparatively early date, probably about the commencement of the reign of Henry II. Mr. Hubert Hall, in *The Athenæum*, advances a fourth opinion, of which we give the following abridgment:—"The city of Winchester was both the natural capital of the West Saxon kingdom, and the place of coronation and burial of West Saxon kings, as well as the official seat of their court and treasury. Here we may suppose such records as existed were placed, these probably including the standard work of Alfred, the Domboc, and those counterparts of charters which served the purpose of a primitive enrolment. And since we know the use made by William I. of Saxon laws and regal customs, we might well conclude that the record of Domesday Survey was deposited at Winchester." But before we can proceed upon this convenient assumption we have to dispose of a direct piece of quasi-contemporary evidence. Ingulphus, Abbot of Croyland, implies that (1) there was a Domesday (Domboc) of Alfred preserved at Winchester and designated as "Rotulus Wintoniæ." (2) The original of the survey of 1086, also called "Rotulus Wintoniæ," was preserved at the same place. (3) The register of Domesday was seen by himself at London, and was consulted there by him, as being doubtless more convenient for reference than the bulky originals at Winchester. Now it is generally proposed to get over this awkward bit of evidence by disparaging the writer's character. True, he was deceitful by his own showing, but not necessarily an untruthful witness of a casual fact. I have not the slightest doubt in my own mind that Ingulphus saw the Domesday register, as it now exists, at Westminster. This, however involves one of two suppositions: either the transfer of the coronation ceremony in Norman times to Westminster has a greater significance than we have imagined, that is to say, as indicating the displacement of Winchester as the financial centre in favour of a new official organisation or pseudo-exchequer at Westminster twenty years before the accepted date; or, as I should prefer to take it, that Winchester continuing the head-quarters of the Treasurer's department and the repository of all the three records referred to by Ingulphus, there is yet every probability that the handy book or register called Domesday followed the Court whenever important business was to be transacted, the original rotulets usually remaining in the Winchester treasury. Thus Domesday Book would often be taken to Westminster, and it is under these circumstances that it would be seen by Ingulphus. But it is important to explain that according to contemporary usage it must have been ultimately returned to its resting-place at Winchester until its services were again called for. This supposition will also clear up the hitherto mysterious passages in the "Annals of Burton" and "Book of Bermondsey," the former of which is said to speak of Domesday as preserved "at Winchester and Westminster," and the latter "at Winchester or Westminster." Mr. Hall goes on to prove, chiefly from a nearly contemporary official record, the "Dialogus de Scaccario," that the origin of the mystery is to be found in the existence of a double treasury, at Winchester and Westminster; while its solution depends on the identification of Domesday, from Henry I. onwards, with one of these, the Westminster. And in support of his propositions he quotes the "Dialogus" as follows:— "(1) That the working records (with the seal and Domesday) were preserved in the Treasury 'Verum plura sunt in repositoriis archis Thesauri . . . qualia sunt sigillum regis . . . *liber judiciarius* . . . et pleraque *alia quæ consedente scaccario quotidianis usibus necessaria sunt.*'—*Dial.* i. 14. (2) That this Treasury was situate in the Exchequer of Receipt: 'Inferius illud scaccarium suas habet personas. . . . *Illic est . . . ostiarius thesauri.*'— *Ibid.* i. 3. (3) That this Exchequer of Receipt was annexed to the Exchequer proper: 'Aliud est inferius, aliud superius (scaccarium); *una tamen origo utriusque.—Ibid.* i. 2. (4) That this Exchequer was at Westminster from ancient times: 'In termino eodem (Michaelis) pro incausto * *totius anni ad utrumque scaccarium*, ij solidi debentur quos sibi *de antique jure* vindicat sacrista majoris ecclesiæ *West-monasterii.*"—*Ibid.* i. 3.

Two interesting items submitted by Andrew Lang:

A CURIOUS TAX.—In 1678 the law required (for purposes of protecting trade) that all the dead should be buried in woollen winding-sheets. The price of the wool was the obolus paid to the Charon of the Revenue. After March 25, 1667, no person was to be "buried in any shirt, shift, or sheet other than should be made of woole only." Thus when the children in a little Oxfordshire village lately beheld a ghost "dressed in a long narrow gown of woollen, with bandages round the head and chin," it is clear that the ghost was much more than a hundred years old, for the Act had fallen into disuse long before it was repealed in 1814. The addition made to the duties of the keeper of the register in 1678 was this—he had to take and record the affidavit of a kinsman of the dead, to the effect that the corpse was actually buried in woollen fabric. The upper classes, however, preferred to bury in linen, and to pay the fine of £5. When Mrs. Oldfield, the famous actress, was interred in 1730, her body was arrayed "in a very fine Brussels lace head-dress, a holland shift, with a tucker and double ruffles of the same lace, and a pair of new kid gloves."

"WELLERISMS."—In a little book called "Wellerisms," the question has been started—what is the origin of those facetious remarks of Sam's which always include the expression, "as" someone or other "said"? "Plenty to get and little to do," as the soldier said when he was sentenced to be flogged. As the judge remarked, "What the soldier said is not evidence." But it is interesting to observe that these facetious *formulæ* are common on the Continent as well as in England, and make part of the traditional wisdom of the people. In French they are called, *Les Comme dits*. In Germany M. E. Holfer has published a collection of them ("Wie das Volk spricht," Stuttgart, 1876, eighth edition). Here are some French examples: "Vive la lumière, comme dit l'aveugle." This answers to, "'I see, I see,' said the blind man." "'You're a liar,' said the dumby"—a refined piece of Scotch popular humour. Here is one from George Sand: "Je vais me résumer, comme dit M. le curé Cuzion au commencement de tous ses sermons." These are Dutch examples: "'I know what I think,' as the madman said to his keeper." "'Nobody to blame,' as the man said when he threw his wife down stairs." "'Excuse me if there is any error,' as the soldier said when he shot his colonel." Sam Weller's *comme dits* are better than these frivolous foreign endeavours.

News and Notes.

Mr. Colnett, proprietor of the new Cock Tavern, has written to *The Times* that all the old fittings, including the celebrated chimney-piece, with the carved oak overmantel, and all the panelling, seats, and tables, have been removed and refitted to the new house over the way.

A German physician has ascertained that the average gain in height during the hours of sleep is five centimetres.

A Common herring with a glass eye is the latest curiosity in natural history, according to *The Fish Trades Gazette.*

Countess Martinengo-Cesaresco communicates to *The Folk-lore Journal* a number of negro songs sung on the Carrington estate in Barbados, and written down by the negroes themselves.[1]

The last person who could converse in the old Cornish dialect was William Bodiner, of Mousehole, according to a correspondent of *The Cornish Telegraph.* Bodiner was a fisherman and died in 1794.

A Lecture on Cremation has been given at Southampton by Mr. F. A. Edwards, from which it appears that the revival of cremation in England was inaugurated by the incineration of the bodies of Lady Dilke and Mrs. Hanham in Dorsetshire in 1882.

1 For more on the Countess, refer to the note on page 106 and her article on page 109.

A Roman coffin and skeleton discovered at Plumstead was buried in the parish churchyard, by orders of the vicar, in spite of the coroner, who claimed jurisdiction over the body, and the local antiquaries, who wished to preserve the coffin.

A clean copy of the original edition of Fielding's "Tom Jones" (1749) is offered for sale by Messrs. Ellis & Scrutton, for six guineas. The same firm have *The Gentleman's Magazine* from its commencement, in 1731, to May, 1868. The set of 228 volumes is offered for £34.

It is not always books with a history that are valued the most highly by the collector of these days. A copy of Milton's "Eikonoklastes," for instance, printed in 1649, in answer to the famous "Eikon Basilike," and afterwards called in by proclamation, and ordered by the Commons to be burnt, is procurable now for about 30s.

The process of Beatification of Sir Thomas More and other martyrs of the Roman Catholic Church in this country is proceeding at Rome; their actual Canonisation will probably follow in due course, several years hence.

The trade of the book-collector—for a trade it has almost become— is not acquired easily. For example, two copies of the Elzevir "Rabelais" were, by a curious chance, picked up on the same day on the same London bookstall. The price of one was a guinea, that of the other was £7 10s. The former was a dear book, the latter was a trouvaille.

The Bishop of St. Albans has consecrated the new nave and chancel of Chigwell Church, Essex. The church, rendered famous by Dickens in his "Barnaby Rudge," has been restored and enlarged at a cost of somewhat exceeding £5,000. The ancient nave becomes the south aisle, and the quaint bell-tower and curious avenue of clipped yews remain as in times past.

The writer of social, literary and scientific articles for the press is said to be a writer of "Middles," or a "Middleman."

The silver snuff-box that once belonged to Mary Lamb, engraven with her name, is now in the possession of Mr. John Hollingshead.

Among the skins used at various times by bookbinders are those of the cat, crocodile, mole, seal, black wolf, royal tiger, otter, white bear, sole, and rattlesnake.

Some Roman remains were discovered a few weeks ago in a large chamber in Poole's Cavern, Buxton. They consisted of a toga, bronze bracelet, a piece of Samian ware, black pottery, charcoal, human remains, and teeth of the wild boar.

Mr. Alexander Brown "will be grateful to anyone for any data or information that may be of value to him" in writing the history of Virginia, with brief biographies of the founders. His address is Norwood Post Office, Nelson County, Virginia, U.S.A.

A lady is said to earn a livelihood by skilfully filling up worm-holes in old books, each leaf being separately and patiently dealt with, the material being chewed or "pulped" and pressed into the hole; the charge is sixpence a hole.

Chapman & Hall's new edition of "The Pickwick Papers" will probably be published on the day of the Queen's accession, and it will contain fac-similes of all the original drawings, including some never yet published.

The Old Mitre Tavern, which used to be one of the favourite resorts of Dr. Johnson and Goldsmith, is now known as the Clachan, and here it was that on the last day of last December over one hundred Scotchmen met to bring in "the New Year."

Mrs. E. Boger will shortly publish "Myths, Scenes, and Worthies of Somerset." Readers of *Walford's Antiquarian* need not to be assured of this lady's qualifications for the task she has undertaken; and those who love the past and the old heroic glories of this realm know that Somerset is classic land, "a good nurse of worthy men," and fruitful in story for the pen of the annalist.[2]

The following anecdote of the late Mr. Solly illustrates one of the

2 For more on Boger, refer to the note on page 106.

difficulties under which the roaming antiquary laboured not fifty years since. Mr. Solly visited Penzance almost half a century ago, and, when thinking of leaving, inquired when the next coach would start, and was informed, in a manner intended to elicit surprise at the frequency of communication with other parts of England, "Oh, sir, it will leave *to-morrow night*."

The twelfth centenary of the death of St. Cuthbert has been celebrated in the Roman Catholic Diocese of Hexham and Newcastle.

In *The Red Dragon* for April there is an article on "Early Welsh Medicine," containing much curious information.

Mr. David Nutt has published a reprint of William Adlington's "Marriage of Cupid and Psyche," by Apuleius. The editor is Mr. Andrew Lang.

The oldest-known manuscript on alchemy, written in Greek in the eleventh century, is about to be printed by M. Berthelot, the eminent chemist, and author of the "Origins of Alchemy."

At the meeting of the British Archæological Association, on April 20, Dr. Harker read a paper on "The Holy Well, Lancaster Castle-hill."

"Flora Day" is to be celebrated at Helston this year, on May 10. It is stated that the "curious customs of the old 'Flora Day' are year by year dwindling in interest.

Mr. Scott-Surtees has propounded a new theory in *Notes and Queries* respecting the Round Table of Arthurian Legend. He is of opinion that King Arthur revived Druidism, and that the Round Table was a kind of High Court of Druids.

No. 1 in the catalogue of the Anglo-Jewish Exhibition is a large bronze ewer, which was found in a Suffolk brook in the seventeenth century. The ewer, which was probably used for some of the ceremonial ablutions connected with the tending of the dead, may be supposed to have been concealed by fugitives immediately before they were driven out from their homes.

Dr. Pitré has published an article in the "archivio per lo Studio delle Tradizioni Popolari" in connection with the Countess E. Martinengo-Cesaresco's communication relative to the practice of beating boys at boundaries. A similar castigation was administered to children in South Italy on the occasion of public executions; the blows fell at the moment when the criminal breathed his last.

In the April number of *The Reliquary* are two articles on the Eucharistic fan or *flabellum*, used in the Eastern Church to drive away flies and to cool the celebrant. Its use became extinct in the Latin Communion during the fifteenth century, with the exception of some churches in *Magna Græcia* and Spain. The flabellum was abolished in the Orthodox Eastern Church about thirty years ago; but the Greek priest still fans his face with his hands while reciting the Creed.

The disinterring of the Sphinx has been going on for more than twelve months, and is now in active progress under M. Grébaut. A flight of steps between the Sphinx and the Pyramid has been uncovered. These steps are mentioned by Pliny, and were uncovered by Caviglia in 1817, but have been entirely lost to sight for nearly seventy years.

An important discovery has been made among the archives of the Jewish community at Corfu. The article discovered is a parchment scroll, containing, however, not the Peutateuch, but the Haptorahs read throughout the year. A note in the handwriting of the scribe indicates that the scroll was written at a time when, in consequence of persecution, the reading of portions from the Prophets was substituted for the reading of the Law. The actual date is believed to be 5020 A. M.

A fete in honour of Rabelais was held in Paris on Whit Sunday.

A copy of the famous "First Folio" of Shakespeare has recently been discovered in an old house in Winchester. The book is in a very dilapidated condition, and Messrs. Zaehnsdorf are at present engaged in restoring it.

A correspondent of *The Manchester City News* gives an account of a strange mirage witnessed by her on April 29. The appearance was that of a church tower rising out of a mass of confused buildings, from which sprang numerous pinnacles.

An account of "English Mediæval Drinking Bowls called Mazers" will be contributed to the fifty-first volume of the *Archæologia* by Mr. St. John Hope.[3]

Shakespeare is the first author that speaks of "the man in the moon," or mentions the potato, or uses the term "eyesore" for annoyance.

Baron de Gostovsky, of Saboucz, near Danzig, who died recently, made the request that at his death his head should be cut off before his interment, a service which he said he had performed on the body of his wife after her death. "We are a family of vampires," he added, "and if this precaution be not taken, we can find no repose in the grave, but come back and bring misfortune to our children."

It appears that among the Greek peasantry the small-pox is known as εὐλογία , or "the blessing," for the same reason that the Black Sea was called the Euxine, or "hospitable" sea.

The Jersey Observer states that the official language of the Channel Island Law Courts is "Norman." We understood that modern French is used in the courts, and should be glad of any communication on this subject.

It is often remarked that in French curé is equivalent to our "vicar," and vicaire to our "curate" At the present day, this is, in a measure, true; but in the Book of Common Prayer "the curate" always means the incumbent of the parish. The "vicar" in mediæval England was usually the deputy of some monastic body, to whom the living had been granted.

A few weeks ago a Devonshire labourer cut his wrist whilst sharpening his scythe. Instead of sending for a doctor his friends called in a man and his wife who have a great repute as "charmers,"

---

3 It is quite possible that Machen read this article. Later, he suggests that the Holy Grail resembles a mazer in *The Sangraal* essays. See *The Great Return* (Darkly Bright, 2017).

and these proceeded to "charm" the wound. It need scarcely be said that the man died of loss of blood shortly after.

A correspondent of *The Pioneer Mail* describes some extraordinary phenomena witnessed by him on May 29. He was called out in the evening by one of his servants to see "what a tamasha was taking place with the star Sook," i.e., Venus. The planet was oscillating violently from left to right, shining brightly and then becoming almost invisible, till the natives thought that the last day was at hand.

A letter, signed Miguel de Cerbantes Saavedra, has lately been discovered in Andalusia. It is dated February 12, 1590, and refers to his duties as a tax collector of the lowest rank.

A work has just appeared which ought to find a place in the libraries of the learned. We refer to an English translation of that collection of mysterious writings known as "Kabbala Denudata"—a collection which possibly Mr. Quaritch may possess in five or six quarto volumes, and value at as many guineas. A hardy Rabbinical scholar, Mr. Mathers, has toiled through these tomes, and the result is a solid volume which may be had through a bookseller for eight shillings.

Pickwick is a local surname. Probably the following is the earliest entry, "William de Pikewike," co. Wilts, A.D. 1273, Hundred Rolls. When at Bath Mr. Pickwick was not far from the home of his ancestors.

The late William Barnes, the "Dorsetshire poet," used to tell of a little boy whom he found one day in a village school, and who had written the word "psalm" in his copybook and then accidentally blotted out the initial "p" with his sleeve. His little sister at his side was in tears at the disaster, but the natural born spelling-reformer defiantly exclaimed: "What if I did scrope of en out? He didn't spell naught, and what was the good of en?"

Mr. Tyler writes to *The Academy* respecting the famous Hittite seal in the possession of Mr. Greville Chester. Mr. Tyler thinks the symbolism on the seal is Pythagorean, and considers it a confirmation of the traditions which tell of the Eastern travels of Pythagoras.

The curious paradox "That Bacon wrote Shakespeare" is receiving vigorous support from the Bacon Society, whose chief object appears to be the establishing of this strange thesis. We refer our readers to the journal of the Society, published in Racquet-court, Fleet-street.

In this connection we may mention that a work entitled 'The Great Cryptogram; or, Francis Bacon's Cipher in the so-called Shakespearean Play," by Mr. Donnelly, will shortly be published in Chicago.

A copy of the first edition of Burton's "Anatomy" fetched £10 15s. at the Randall sale.[4]

An interesting discussion took place on the recent visit of the Archæological Institute to Stonehenge. One of the speakers advanced the prehistoric temple theory, while Mr. Arthur Evans assigned B.C. 450 as the probable date of erection. He was led to this conclusion by finding an amber necklace in an adjacent barrow; the amber being proved to be coëval with certain Greek vases of known date.

Dr. Cox, on the other hand, contended that 450 A.D. was a likelier date, stating that he had found a Roman tile beneath an immense stone of similar character at Carnac, in Brittany. He considered Stonehenge as "a combined sepulchre and military trophy, set up by a great company of victorious troops."

The Vicar of Amesbury, who advocated the solar theory, and stated that he himself had seen the sun rise, on the longest day, immediately over the "Friar's Heel" stone, seems to have been treated with some contempt. He was reminded that he could see the sun rise over any gate-post, if he took up the right position.

Considerable discussion has arisen with regard to a phrase used by Dr. Johnson. "At the altar," says the Doctor, "I recommended my θ φ." Croker interprets these letters by θνητοὶ φίλοι, "departed friends," which, of course, is not Greek at all, θνητός meaning "mortal." But

---

4 Burton's *Anatomy* is mentioned at the conclusion of The Novel of The Iron Maid segment of Machen's *The Three Imposters* (1895).

there can be no doubt that "dead friends" is the meaning of the letters; and a writer in *The Academy* has propounded the theory that the θ stands for "dead," it being a recognised symbol, among Greeks and Romans, in the physician's case-book, and the muster-roll of an army. It is, however, an abbreviation not of θνητός, "mortal," but of θάνατος, "death."

In the country, the composer of epitaphs occasionally gives way to strange flights of fancy. At Foile, Sussex, there is a tombstone "erected to the memory of Thomas Budget . . . who was drowned . . . whilst fishing, in the 21st year of his age by his sorrowing parents!"

In the July number of *Walford's Antiquarian* we gave the receipt for "mum." The celebrated "Athole Brose" is simpler in concoction, being made simply of equal quantities of whiskey, dripped honey, and thick cream thoroughly mixed together.[5]

Mr. Labouchere is reported to have said during a debate in the House of Commons that the office of Lion-King-at-Arms was a sinecure, and that heraldry was a ridiculous relic of past ages.

We would recommend Mr. Labouchere to subscribe to Dr. Howard's *Miscellanea Genealogica et Heraldica* (140, Wardour-street), and hear the other side of the question. In fact, we commend the *Miscellanea* to all our readers who care at all for heraldry. The occasional reproductions of illuminated grants of arms are beautifully executed.

A strange anthropological discovery is reported to have been made in the Eastern Pyrenees. In the valley of Ribas a race of dwarfs, called by the people "Nanos," is said to exist. They never attain more than four feet in height, and have high cheek bones and almond eyes of the Mongolian type. They marry only amongst themselves, and are of a very low intellectual type.[6]

At the dissolution of the monasteries, agriculture was neglected, and

5 For this more on this topic, see page 86.

6 This item is intriguing when considering Machen's Turanian twist on the Little People. For more, refer to notes on pages 33 and 45.

there can be no doubt that the poor often longed for the old days. A song of the day runs thus:—

I'll tell thee what, good vellowe,
Before the Vriars went hence,
A Bushel of the best wheate
Was sold for vourteen pence;
And vorty eggs a penny.

A strange case was heard some time ago before the Queen's Bench. A firm of metal-workers received an order for some angels for artistic iron gates, intended to stand at the late Lord Dudley's seat, near Whitby. The angels (which are the supporters of the Dudley arms) are described as being so "questionable and improperly draped" that Lady Dudley had them immediately removed. Hence a lawsuit on the artistic merits of the angels.

At the Reformation the English bishops dropped the phrase "Dei gratia" from their seals, though retaining it in documents. Bishop Wordsworth, of Salisbury, has restored the words on his new seal.

A curious marriage custom is observed in the town of Knutsford, in Cheshire. Patterns in white sand are traced on the street cobbles before the house wherein is the marriage feast. There is, of course, a legend referring the custom to a circumstance in the life of Knut, but we imagine that some of our readers might offer a better explanation of the rite.

The inscriptions discovered at Gortyna, in Crete, date from before the introduction of money into Greece. The standards of value mentioned are the caldron and the tripod, or three-footed kettle.

At Pirton Church, in Hertfordshire, a bell is rung at nine o'clock, for no obvious reason. It is stated on somewhat doubtful authority to be a survival of the nine o'clock mass.

It is stated that the two castles of Arundel and Abergavenny confer the title of Earl on their possessors. How is this to be understood? Would a commoner, on purchasing Arundel Castle, become Earl of Arundel?

As late as 1638 flowers were bought for dressing the parish church of Newbury, in Berkshire. In George Herbert's famous "Country Parson," decking with boughs is enjoined, on the great festivals, but no mention is made of flowers.

The historical Robin Hood's or St. Ann's Well at Nottingham has just been destroyed for the formation of a railway. It was situated in Sherwood Forest, and the first name is said to be the original one. From the earliest times it was celebrated for its supposed healing properties, which, no doubt, was the real cause of the erection of a chapel near it in 1409, dedicated to St. Ann, the priests of which demanded a fee for the use of the waters.

A most interesting paper on the name "Weeping Cross" is contained in The East Anglian for August. Mr. W. H. Sewell, the writer, conjectures that a "weeping cross" was a cross by the wayside, where the mourners in a funeral procession were accustomed to rest, and to say a *De Profundis* for the dead.

A duel with cross-bows has lately been fought at Paris.

The first detailed account of tobacco in the English language is believed to be (smokers, mark the title): "Joyfull newes oute of the newe founde world. Englished by John Frampton, Marchant. London, 1577."

Inventors are often subject to opprobrium. In 1312 a certain chaplain of Ripon, who seems not to have been leading a regular life, was charged with having invented a pestiferous game called "Dyngethryftes," which had become very seductive to his neighbours. To "ding" in the northern dialects means to drive down or to throw with violence. So this new game, so long forgotten, probably had some relation to quoits or pitching the bar.

A series of subterranean passages was opened up, and in them were found numerous objects of interest. Not the least interesting was a red granite tomb dated 1509, some bronze armour, several fowling-pieces, a richly embossed lamp, and a large quantity of vellum manuscripts. Unfortunately, however, there appears to be no vestige of truth in the story, which must take its place beside other antiquarian hoaxes.

We are pleased to find that the Bladigdone Brass, so long missing from East Wickham Church, Kent, has been discovered; the parts of the cross which were gone when the late Rev. H. Haines published his valuable manual have been restored, and the whole relaid, together with a small inscription plate recording the fact of the restoration.

Mr. F. C. Eden writes:— "In your 'News and Notes' of September, you mention that a bell is rung at nine o'clock at Pirton Church, Herts. It may interest your readers to know that a like custom survives at Minestead, which is the mother church of Lyndhurst, a village of some celebrity in the New Forest."

Additional Antiquarian Articles

Editor's Note

The following items have been included to provide further opportunities in experiencing the eclectic charm of *Walford's Antiquarian*.

The first example is likely a contribution by the magazine's publisher, George Redway.

Evelyn Lillian Haseldine Carrington, Countess Martinengo-Cesaresco (1852-1931) was a noted historian and folklorist. She was a regular contributor to the magazine.

Samuel Barber remains obscure as the name is a common one. Apparently, this Barber followed in the tradition of many English clergymen by spending his spare time in antiquarian pursuits.

Charlotte Gilson Boger (1826-1903), the wife of a clergyman, wrote a single novel before turning to nonfiction. In this capacity, she became a noted antiquarian by publishing books such as *Myths, Scenes and Worthies of Somerset* (see page 95). She is likely the author of the first unsigned article, while the author of the last article remains unidentified.

The Romance of a Gibbet.

June 1887, pp. 400-401

Washwood Heath, 2½ miles east of Birmingham, was formerly the chief place of execution near that town. As such it witnessed many a terrible sight; none more terrible, perhaps, than that of eight men hanging at once (none of them for murder, several for petty offences), on April 19, 1802, in the presence of 100,000 persons. But it has its romance, unchronicled, and forgotten of most.

On Wednesday, November 22, 1780, two soldiers belonging to recruiting parties in Birmingham procured a brace of pistols, and set out to rob on the Coleshill road. They were Corporal Thomas Pitmore, a Cheshire rake, who had enlisted after spending a fortune of £700, and John Hamond, drummer, a born American. Between seven and eight o'clock at night they made an attempt on two horsemen, the foremost members of a party of Birmingham butchers, returning from Rugby fair. Pitmore grasped the bridle of the first man, a Mr. Rose, whose horse, however, started and ran away. The drummer then presented his pistol at the second traveller, Mr. Wilfrid Barwick, crying "stop your horse," but his own agitation caused him to discharge the weapon before the unfortunate man could comply. A third butcher, Mr. Rann, hearing the report, rode forward followed by his servant, and, seeing Barwick on the ground, and a man making off across a field, leapt the hedge, and gave chase. The fellow turned and presented his pistol, but, having lost the ramrod, knew that it would be useless to fire. The other butchers arriving with their servants, he gave himself up, and informed on his accomplice Pitmore, who was apprehended the same night at his lodgings in Birmingham, whither he had escaped. Poor Barwick was carried to a neighbouring public-house, where he died in ten minutes, with three slugs in his body. One had forced its way almost through him, and was found wrapped in a piece of his shirt, another had entered the groin, the third severed an artery, causing internal bleeding and death.

The trial of the culprits took place March 31, 1781, and they were sentenced to be hanged on the Heath, and their bodies exhibited in chains near the scene of the murder. This was accordingly done on April 2. A vast concourse assembled to witness the event, for the men were familiarly known throughout the district as "Tom" and "Joe." Just before they were swung off they turned their ghastly faces towards each other, and the Corporal said "Good-bye, Tom," to which the drummer replied "Good-bye, Joe."

Their bodies swung, and rattled, and rotted in the air for many a day, but disappeared one night, leaving no traces.[1] This event was a topic for years. But another generation sprang up, and another, and the affair was gradually forgotten. But "murder will out," and to all eternity. On a Thursday morning, January, 1842, sixty-two years after the crime, some navvies employed in a field near Washwood Heath, were removing a quantity of earth for the Birmingham and Derby railway, when they discovered two skeletons environed in chains. Again the tongues wagged, and the old tale was retold, and an enterprising publican of the place secured the chains, and exhibited the same to curious callers. Alas! Tom and Joe. By the irony of fate their own dry bones had come to light to blazon their crime anew.

GEORGE.

---

1 Since the above copy was sent in, the writer of this article has had some conversation with one familiar with the object and operation of removal. The unsightly burden of the gibbet was the one eyesore in a lovely view from a neighbouring hall, and the proprietor hired certain men to inter the remains. The men went to an adjacent field, and, carefully cutting out a square of turf, dug a deep pit. So that no traces should be left, they took with them a large rick-sheet, on which turf and soil were laid. The bodies were then taken from the gibbet, and placed in the hole; as much of the soil as could be forced in was returned, the turf was evenly replaced, and the remaining soil was carried away in the sheet, and distributed over a distant tract of waste land.

ꬰolk-lore of British Birds.

March 1887, pp. 158-160

The Rev. C. Swainson has produced a work[1] which ought not only to be welcomed by antiquarians and students of folk-lore, but also to have a place assigned to it in the library of every country house in the kingdom. The old rustic names of our British birds maybe doomed to oblivion, but they are still sufficiently a part of the living speech of the people to have been constantly heard by anyone who has lived long in the country, and in many this collection of them will awaken pleasant memories of childhood, when we ourselves should have said that we had been to look at the mavis' nest, or that the cushat had been heard in the wood. The rural names are often happily descriptive, and if at times they show a droll endeavour to imitate the cry or song of the bird, at others they are more poetic, both in sound and sense, than the approved term. The habit of rustics of imagining a likeness between the cry of a bird and some word or name with which they are familiar is illustrated by a case which comes within our own recollection. The labourers working on a glebe farm where there was a large rookery were firmly convinced that one of the rooks, which cawed in a shrill, peculiar manner, was constantly repeating "Parker!" that being the name of one of their number.

A mere list of local names would have been of great value, but Mr. Swainson's book is much more than this. With much industry and judgment, he has arranged in a readable form the chief superstitions and legends, both English and foreign, which are attached to each bird. Some birds owe a large debt of gratitude to popular prejudice, which has gone all in their favour; others, on the contrary, have been from time immemorial so evilly spoken of and so persistently persecuted that it is a wonder if their species still survives. First among the former class is, of course, the robin. We do not altogether agree with the author when he says, "The respect with which the robin is regarded throughout Europe is probably

---

1 *The Folk-lore and Provincial Names of British Birds.*

due to its colour." Surely the fact that he is the tamest and most sociable of all wild birds counts for something in the affection which he engenders, though it may be argued that his tameness is simply the hereditary consequence of the good treatment he has received. We are sorry to say that this good treatment by no means extends "throughout Europe." In Italy robins may be seen hanging up for sale in the poulterers' shops with all the other little feathered victims. The only bird which is looked upon as in any way sacred in Italy is, so far as we know, the swallow, which is dedicated to the Madonna. In general, sacred birds will be found to have two sets of legends, one of great antiquity, the other of Christian origin. The latter set represents them as having rendered some service to our Saviour on the way to Calvary, or on the Cross. By the earlier legends they are distinguished as fire-bearers, and hence are sacred to the god Donar. In their connection with fire was seen the cause of the robin's red breast and the woodpecker's red head. It seems singular that amongst the rewards promised to the robin in a Breton story quoted by Mr. Swainson we read, "blue as heaven shall be thy eggs;" as everyone knows that the bird's eggs are not blue, and the mistake is of a kind rarely found in folk-lore. We may just notice, too, that we have some doubts as to whether the singing-bird mentioned in the Chippeway story (p. 13) was really a robin, as we have always understood that the American bird which bears that name can hardly utter a note.

One bird is alike the object of honour and persecution. "The wren, the wren, the king of birds," is unquestionably a lightning bird, sacred to Donar; but, like some other crowned heads, it pays dearly for its rank. The hunting of the wren on Christmas Day is one of the old customs which we would most gladly see abandoned, but which is still extant over a large part of Europe. It is certain that the practice recalls some ancient sacrificial rite, and that it is based on the idea, so strongly rooted in all early communities, that the most esteemed, the most valuable person or thing should be chosen for sacrifice. In modern times, after the boys have slain the wren, they take it round, as an excuse for asking for largess, as Greek children did, and do, take round the swallow; a fact mentioned by the author, though he omits to state that the jackdaw was also carried about in the same fashion in ancient Greece.

Owls and the crow tribe have been placed almost universally without the pale of human sympathy. It is wonderful what cruel and cowardly acts even educated persons have been known to commit under the influence of the superstitious fear inspired by these birds. Some years ago it was recorded in the biography of a well-known man of letters that he actually killed, or caused to be killed, a tame raven which he imagined "looked" at him. Somewhat similar is the following story, for which we can vouch: In 1852 Victor Emanuel's Queen (an Austrian Princess) spent some time at the Hotel Croce di Malta at Spezia. The proprietor had two favourite crows, which the Queen so much disliked that she induced him to send them away. At first, they were taken to short distances, but they always came back; then they were taken to Sardinia, but they returned home again. After that, the poor things were hidden away in a place of confinement, where, before very long, they died.

In conclusion, it may be worth while to point out that in saying that Dante observed the habit of the lark of dropping to the earth at the end of its song, Mr. Swainson has been led astray by a mistranslation. Dante does not say that the lark drops to earth, but that it remains silent, satiate with sweetness. The beautiful lines, which were so dear to Walter Savage Landor, run thus:—

"Qual lodoletta, che in aere si spazia,
Prima cantando, e poi tace contenta
Dell' ultima dolcezza che la sazia."

E. Martinengo-Cesaresco.

Arthur Machen

The Romans in Cumbria.

April 1887, pp. 259-263

This village of Seascale, entirely a "new" place to modern travellers, was apparently, in very early days, inhabited by and familiar to our Celtic ancestors. Not to speak of the Druidical stones which were lately to be seen between Seascale and Sellafield, and one of which still remains above ground, it is probable that a British village stood formerly at Seascale, upon the ground occupied by the little iron church, and the higher ground called the "Banks."

It is a fact well known to archæologists that a Roman villa stood near the coast, a few miles away, towards Ravenglass; and, as Roman remains are so often associated with British, it may interest antiquaries to know that the present writer found, a year or two ago, in the floor of the little church at Haile, near Egremont, a Roman memorial tablet with a dedication as follows:—

DI BVS

HERCVLI

E. T.

SILVANO.

F. T.

Attention has also been drawn to the iron slag in the bank of a meadow as evidence of ancient work done at Wastdale, about six miles from Seascale. These latter remains must have been either Roman or Celtic, and similar indications of the industry of those distant times are reported as occurring near Whitehaven and Cleator.

In the time of the Roman occupation, and earlier, the lower lands and the dales of Cumberland were probably much more populated than a casual traveller would imagine; more so than the nature of the country would at first lead us to think; and this remark applies, I think, especially to the coast. Take, for example, the district of Millom, on the estuary of the Duddon. Till the development, in quite recent days, of the valuable iron workings at Hodbarrow, this must have remained for centuries a very quiet and sparsely populated district. Yet the Celtic and Druidical remains of still earlier times are abundant, and worthy of careful study.

Both at Kirksanton, a small mining village near Millom (apparently of great antiquity), and on the higher ground following the course of the Duddon, the Druids seem to have had their meeting grounds and cemeteries,[1] and a British town is said to have lain beneath the shadow of Black Comb.

For the present, however, I return to Seascale, to observe that the Roman road (which must have run along the coast here, from the Furness district and Lancaster, to Whitehaven and the iron workings at Cleator) appears to have collapsed by the advance of high water mark and the consequent crumbling of the cliffs. A considerable slice has been added to the shore from the cliff at Seascale within the memory of living inhabitants, or, at any rate, during the last two generations. This falling away of cliffs is no doubt irregular in its effects, and results in a change of form to the coast line, as well as an actual loss of land, won by the encroaching tide. It has always seemed unlikely to the writer that the Roman camp at Maryport (well known from the extraordinary number and preservation of the memorial altars found there) should have been laid down in a position so insecure and so near the edge of the bank. Indeed, an examination of this bank, a little to the north of the camp, will lead to the conclusion that not only fields but gardens and villas have at that point fallen down to the beach.

And I would direct the attention of those interested in the Roman positions to the coast line in the outskirts of Seascale and the road between that place and Drigg. The fact of a villa having stood near Ravenglass, and that of the Celtic remains being so numerous in the neighbourhood of Millom, Kirksanton, and the Duddon, renders it highly probable that one important Roman station, at least, was situated between the Duddon and St. Bees. This station would, there is reason to believe, be near the coast. Like the monks of the middle ages, these adventurous warriors appreciated bold scenery and fresh sea breezes; and, as it was their custom to establish stations and camps to counteract the rebellious designs of the conquered race, their fortresses may be looked for in such positions as naturally correspond with the British rallying places. This has been pointed out by antiquaries who have examined the Midland district. And

---

1 A pair of long stones, locally termed the "Giant's Grave," stand yet in stately solemnity near this village.

it is almost certain that there were numerous Celtic strongholds on the high lands by the Duddon, near Black Comb, on Irton Fells, Wastdale Screes, and so on, to Dent, Whitehaven, and the iron district above referred to.[2] I would therefore venture to suggest to archæologists a more careful exploration of the neighbourhood of Seascale, Sellafield, and Nethertown, for the site of a camp in this district. It is more than probable that the Romans would keep near the sea in their first inroads into these parts.

I will now describe one or two features of the coast, which were observed by me during a recent visit. The crumbling away of the cliff at Seascale is most noticeable about the railway station, where there is a kind of inlet, or break in the coast line. The straight road which runs from Drigg to Seascale appears to end at the bridge on the Drigg side of Seascale, for we cannot suppose that the curve which there bends to the sea is part of the original road. Whether it ran in the line of the Furness Railway, and continued, on the edge of the cliff past the site of the station;[3] or whether it turned inland, cannot perhaps be decided from an examination of the Seascale district alone; but let the archæologist proceed along the bank by the sea for about 100 yards past the station, to where a brook runs upon the beach. Just on the other side of the inlet formed by the brook, and between the line and the edge of the cliff, are to be found blocks of stone, laid in line, and running almost parallel with the railway line. These might be thought of little importance by themselves; but on the other side of the railway line, close to the fence, may be found other blocks of stone,[4] parallel, or nearly so, to the first mentioned. The space between the two sets of stones is slightly in excess of that occupied by the line; that is, about the same as an ordinary Roman road, but rather less than that of Watling Street, or the greater roads. In noting this width, it seemed probable to me that the two stone fences abutted on a road of one kind or other. It would be interesting to make a full examination of this place, with a view to pointing out the advance of the sea, as well as showing the nature of the building that evidently existed here.

2 Since writing the above I find that there was a Roman station at Muncaster.

3 This seems quite improbable, as the centres of population would be near Whitehaven and Egremont, and Roman roads were usually as scraight as possible.

4 Let me warn visitors that mineral trains are frequent on this line.

The part of the common just above the Banks might, I think, also repay investigation. The mounds and loose stones here and there have a very artificial cast.

The last remark applies also to one or two places in the neighbourhood of Haile, the village where the altar above referred to was found. Space will not now permit me, however, to refer at any length to this place. I will merely mention that, while residing in the vicarage a few years ago, I observed, in the meadow which adjoins the end of the vicarage garden, a wide, straight line in the grass, marking the site, and probably the foundation, of a strong wall. The place is almost level, and I should not have observed the lines but for the differentiated melting of the hoar frost. Taken in connection with the altar dedicated to Hercules and Silvanus, this is suggestive. A tradition exists of a battle fought here.

In concluding this paper, I may notice the existence of remains of a monastic house at Beckermet, two miles from Haile, and Calder Abbey, within an easy walk.

Rev. Samuel Barber.

𝔖𝔦𝔯 𝔖𝔞𝔤𝔢𝔰 𝔬𝔣 𝔖𝔬𝔪𝔢𝔯𝔰𝔢𝔱.

June 1887, pp. 365-369

A goodly band they were in those days hailing from Somerset. The summer-land then put forth rich flowers of rhetoric, and ripe fruits of learning and science, too rich and ripe to be allowed to remain to adorn their own county; and so, of these great men, one alone, and he the least known, stayed to work in his own land: this was Maurice Somerset. But we will take them in order.

It is strange that of the two most noted in their day, Adelard of Bath and Roger Bacon, Fuller omits any mention in his "Book of Worthies."

Adelard of Bath lived not long after the first Crusade; those Quixotic, and yet not fruitless, expeditions, which, though they missed the object they had at heart, yet brought back new impulses to thought and learning. Some of this knowledge, which at that time was rife in the East, but strange in our barbarous Western land, seems to have been amongst the Jews, who established schools at which even Christians (who had a craving for knowledge beyond the narrow routine of ecclesiastical teaching) studied; and it is likely enough that from one of them Adelard learned that the knowledge and science unknown to Northern Europe were to be gathered in Egypt and Arabia, and in the Mahommedan schools of Bagdad and Cordova. At any rate, whatever may have given the first impulse, Adelard went on his travels; and gathering learning wherever he went, he stored it up in the cells of his mind, till he could use it for the advantage of the busy hive of Oxford scholars.

He seems principally to have affected the study of mathematics; he translated Euclid's Elements from Arabic into Latin, before any Greek copies had been discovered. He also translated and wrote several other treatises on mathematical and medical subjects, which remain in manuscript in the libraries of Corpus Christi and Trinity Colleges, Oxford. In fact, he appears to have introduced the study of mathematics into the University. The philosophers of the next century owed their greatness in a considerable degree to the impulse given by Adelard's travels in search of knowledge and thought.

Next in order of time comes Maurice Somerset—or, as one

would suppose, Maurice of Somerset. "Born," says Fuller, "in Somersetshire, a Cistercian in Ford Abbey, and bred in Oxford, was Abbot of Wells."

This peculiar designation of Somerset, the county, instead of the parish, in which he was born, may be accounted for thus: Ford Abbey (the name of which still remains attached to what is left of the old building, converted now, with modern additions, into a fine country seat) stands so exactly at the junction of the three counties of Somerset, Devon, and Dorset, that it is claimed by each in turn; any brother of the monastery who was attached to his own county might well therefore, choose to be known by it, as else it might be a matter of doubt to which he belonged. How Maurice Somerset could be Abbot of Wells, when there was no monastery there, requires explanation. Wells had a college for canons; he may possibly have been head of it. He flourished about 1193.

Next to him we must place Robert Bacon, a brother, or, as some think, an uncle of Roger Bacon. He flourished at the same time, and was a noted preacher, and was appointed to preach before Henry III. He, too, was a Franciscan Friar. But his relative, Roger Bacon, was one of those who, if none other of note had lived in his time, was enough of himself to make the century famous. He studied science deeply, and seems to have adopted the friar's dress as a cloak to shield him in his prosecution of what was then generally considered the black art. His investigations and discoveries were constantly hindered both by persecution and want of means; at last, he secured a patron in the reigning Pontiff, Clement IV., and it is to this patron's verbal encouragement we owe his "Opus Majus." "But," says Green, in his "History of the English People," "it was its own great reward; not even a word of acknowledgment seems to have reached him. Some say he gained but a prison." "Unheard, unforgotten, buried," the old man died as he had lived; and it has been reserved for later years to roll away the obscurity that had gathered round his memory, and to place first in the great roll of modern science the name of Roger Bacon."[1]

---

1 It is worthy of remark that Hugh of Wells (not "S." Hugh of Avalon), who had been promoted from being Archdeacon of Wells to the Bishopric of Lincoln, was Robert Grostete's first patron, who, in his turn, was the friend and in some sort the patron of the two Somersetshire men, Roger Bacon and Adam de Marisco. We are told that Robert Grostete's profound learning won the admiration of Roger Bacon, and that it was by Grostete's counsel that he assumed the Franciscan habit.

One of Bacon's uncanny works was supposed to be his magic glass, evidently a distorted report of the telescope, which it seems certain that he discovered.

Two Oxford scholars, both sons of Suffolk squires, request Bacon to allow them to see, in his magic glass, how their fathers, who are friends, fare. They are seated, and in the glass, which is supposed to fill the back of the stage, appear the fathers of the two young men, but alas! they are quarrelling violently, a fight ensues, and they kill each other; whereupon the scholars, to avenge their parents, attack each other, and die also.

After this tragedy, Bacon, much shocked, destroys his magic glass, and forswears necromancy for evermore.

This play only represents the strange ideas held in the middle ages of one whose learning and science was too great for the ignorance of the times to understand, and who appears to have anticipated the discoveries of modern times with so strange a prevision, and so to have accumulated experiment upon experiment that it was but the gross stupidity of the times that prevented Roger Bacon from anticipating the fame of Francis Bacon or of Isaac Newton. But one thing seems certain, Francis Bacon borrowed, unacknowledged, much of his philosophy which has made him so famous from his earlier namesake, the philosopher of Somerset.[2]

Fuller mentions so highly Alexander of Essebie, and so unhesitatingly places him amongst the worthies of Somerset, that we cannot omit him here. He says of him:—

"Alexander of Essebie, the prince of English poets in his age, put our English Festivals into verse, and wrote the History of the Bible, with the lives of some Saints, in an heroic poem. He became Prior of Essebay Abbey, and flourished under Henry III., 1220."

Essebie or Ashby is in Northamptonshire; it seems probable therefore that he was of obscure birth in Somerset, and only became known after he had become settled in Northamptonshire.

Last, but not least of all, let us mention reverently Adam de Marisco, the friend of the two greatest men of his age, Bacon and Grostête. Adam de Marisco, or Adam Marsh, was born, says

2 It was a pitiful thing for two such great men as Francis Bacon and Milton to have allowed themselves to be detected in such literary thefts. Milton, who was a great Anglo-Saxon scholar, owed as much to Cœdman, the poet of Whitby, as Lord Bacon did to Roger.

Fuller, probably at Brent Marsh. He was D.D. of Oxford. Robert Grostête and he jointly compared the Scriptures; being afterwards a Franciscan Friar at Worcester, he furnished the library there with excellent manuscripts. He flourished about 1257. Hugo de Belsham, his corrival, is said to have got the Bishopric of Ely from him.

He was buried in Lincoln Cathedral, close by the side of his friend and fellow student, Hugh Grostête. He lies between him and the wall. They were lovely in their lives, and in their death they were not divided.

Dr. Stubbs calls the reign of Henry III. the golden age of English Churchmanship; is it not also the golden age of mediæval philosophy? and was not its birthplace in Somerset?

Arthur Machen

The Resting-Place of Cromwell.

December 1887, pp. 277-282

The question of the final disposal of the remains of the great Protector is one which, it is believed, has never been set at rest, so that it may not be uninteresting to reproduce the various views which have been, with greater or less persistency, maintained on a subject which has ever presented a fruitful field for inquiry and discussion.

It was on the 3rd of September, 1658, the eve of the anniversary of Dunbar and of the crowning mercy of Worcester—a day which Cromwell had ever annually celebrated with praise and thanksgiving—that, between three and four o'clock in the afternoon, the Protector breathed his last. The corpse was embalmed, wrapped in six folds of cere-cloth, and placed in an inner shell of lead and a strong wooden coffin. It was necessary that it should be buried, as contemporary accounts phrase it, *out of hand.* Before, however, entering upon the much-disputed question of what was actually done with it, it will probably be most convenient to trace briefly the narrative of events connected with the funeral, which gave rise to a spectacle unquestionably one of the most splendid and imposing which England has ever witnessed. The ceremony was fixed originally for the 9th of November, but was postponed to the 23rd. On the 26th of September, the coffin (though the corpse had been immediately buried) was privately removed from Whitehall to Somerset House, where an effigy of the late Protector was exhibited lying in state. The effigy reposed on a raised bed, around which wax tapers encircled it with never-failing rays—a halo of light and glory; and over the bed an inscription was set up, reciting the various vicissitudes through which Oliver Cromwell had risen from a captain of horse to be Lord Protector, and setting forth his triumphs from the time that he was made commander-in-chief to the then recent surrender of Dunkirk. On the 23rd of November the effigy was taken down and laid on an open chariot, to be borne from Somerset House through streets lined with soldiers, railed in and strewn with sand, to the great temple of silence and reconciliation—Westminster Abbey. This was the ceremony which Evelyn witnessed and described "as the joyfullest funeral that ever he saw," for "there were none that cried but dogs, which the soldiers hooted away with as barbarous noise, drinking and taking tobacco in the streets as they went." Cowley, too, was there; "the hearse," he says, "was magnificent, the idol crowned, but yet the whole was so managed as to represent somewhat the life of him for whom it was made; much noise, much tumult, much expense, much magnificence, much vain glory: briefly a great show, but an ill sight." Now, it will be borne in mind that, despite the process of embalmment which it had undergone, the body was in a condition to necessitate immediate burial, and that it had been consigned to the tomb prior to the great procession of the 23rd of November. While it admits of no question that there has been, from the very first, a degree of mystery shrouding the immediate disposition of the body, the probabilities point to the correctness of the view that it was, at any rate, originally buried in Henry VII.'s Chapel, though, as regards its final resting-place, after exhumation, a wide field for speculation is open. It has been said that, by the Protector's own order, the interment took place on the battlefield of Naseby; others, again, have asserted that the body was wrapped in lead and sunk in the deepest part of the Thames. A tradition is said to exist that it was borne, shortly after death, to the village of Northborough, Northamptonshire, and there buried secretly by night; and it has been contended, with at least equal certainty, that Newburgh Hall, in the North Riding of Yorkshire, contains the last resting-place of the great Protector. Nor, again, have there been wanting those who have seen good reason for believing that the remains were conveyed for burial to the immediate neighbourhood of Huntingdon; and there formerly existed a favourite tradition among the inhabitants of Red Lion Square and its vicinity that the body of Oliver Cromwell was buried in the centre of their square, beneath an obelisk which stood there until within a few years.

Amid much that is uncertain and contradictory, we shall tread upon firmer ground when we come to examine the circumstances connected with the exhumation of the body by order of the House of Commons, Saturday, January 26, 1661. Cromwell's corpse was then found wrapped in green cere-cloth in a vault at the east end of the middle aisle of Henry VII.'s Chapel, and which, many years afterwards, was still called Oliver's, or Cromwell's, Vaults. Upon the breast, enclosed in a thin leaden case, was a finely gilt copper plate, bearing on one side the arms of England impaled with those of Cromwell, and on the reverse this legend: "Oliverius protector reipublicæ Angliæ, Scotia et Hiberniæ, natus 25 April. 1599, inauguratus 16 Dec., 1653, mortuus 3 Sep., ann. 1658. Hic situs est." This plate was shown to the Society of Antiquaries, 1738, by Dr. Cromwell Mortimer, whose father married the daughter of Richard Cromwell, and in 1773 was in possession of the Honourable George Hobart, of Norton, Lincolnshire, and is believed to be now in the hands of the Marquis of Ripon. Dr. Mortimer likewise saw the original receipt of the mason employed to open the vaults of Cromwell, Ireton, and Bradshaw, to the following effect: "May the fourth day 1661 received then in full of the worshipful Serjeant Norfolke (of the House of Commons) fifteen shillings for taking up the corpses of Cromwell, Ireton and Bradshaw, received by me, John Lewis." The Monday night following the exhumation, the bodies of Cromwell and Ireton were drawn on separate carts to the Red Lion Inn, Holborn, a proceeding the necessity for which does not appear, but in connection with which it has been stated that Cromwell's body was at that time interred in a small adjacent paddock. The remains were, at any rate, detained the 28th and 29th at the inn, a time sufficiently long to have enabled those who wished to preserve them from insult to substitute another body. On the 30th of January, according to the usually received account, the bodies were conveyed on sledges to Tyburn, and after having been suspended on a gallows from morning until four o'clock, were beheaded, the trunks buried on the spot, and the heads set up on poles on the roof of Westminster Hall. From the word *Tyburn* being so distinctly made use of in connection with the narrative of this occurrence, it has been usually assumed that the well-known place for executing criminals, near the north end of Park Lane, is intended to be designated. It is, however, worthy of note that for nearly two centuries the Holborn end of Fetter Lane, which is within a short distance of Red Lion Square, was no less frequently the place of execution. In conveying the bodies to the Red Lion Inn, Holborn, the Government might have had in view the proximity of the house to the scaffold and the scene of the disgusting exhibition on the anniversary of King Charles's death.

We are now in a position better adapted for judging of the amount of credibility which may probably be assigned to the various stories which have been circulated as to the final burial-place of Cromwell. As regards the locality of Naseby field, it has been said that Barkstead, the regicide, Lieutenant of the Tower, desiring to know during his last illness where the Protector wished to be buried, received the answer, "as nigh as can be guessed to the spot where the heat of the action was at Naseby." In accordance with the desire thus expressed, the body was conveyed thither in a hearse, attended by young Barkstead, a boy of about fifteen years of age, who is said to have stated that on reaching Naseby, a grave was found prepared, in which the coffin was placed, and that the ground was speedily ploughed over and sown with corn. In corroboration of this view, a former Rector of Naseby is said to have ascertained from Mr. Henry Cromwell, of Cheshunt (great-grandson of Henry Cromwell, Lord Deputy of Ireland), who died 1821, that his mother, who lived to the age of 103 years, had been told by a servant of Richard Cromwell's that he could well remember the fact of Oliver's body passing through Cheshunt by night, and further, that he accompanied it as far as Huntingdon, but that the hearse was taken further on. Mr. Cromwell is reported to have added that the tradition among the Protector's immediate descendants had ever been that he was buried in a field on his estate near Huntingdon. The claims of Newburgh Hall, the seat of Sir George Wombwell, and formerly of the Fauconbergs in the North Riding of Yorkshire, and the depository of many Cromwellian relics, including the Protector's sword, watch, and saddle, yet remain to be noticed. Mary Cromwell was the second wife of the second Lord Fauconberg, and is said to have inherited no small amount of her father's capacity. Foreseeing in the Protector's death the earliest streak of the Restoration dawn, and the future dishonour of her father's remains, she caused the corpse to be removed from its original resting place in the Abbey (a substitution being made), and arranged for its secret removal to Newburgh Hall, where, in a secluded part of the upper apartments, an enormous mass of brickwork, cemented into the walls, is reported to be the actual tomb of the Protector. A tradition to this effect has, at any rate, been preserved in the Bellasis family during two centuries and a quarter.

Whatever impression, however, be formed as to the ultimate disposal of Cromwell's body, there appear no grounds for doubting that, shortly after death, it was buried in Henry VII.'s chapel. There existed no reason indeed why the Protector should anticipate that any indignity would be offered to his remains; on the contrary, he died in the full conviction that he had accomplished a great work, and it is but reasonable to suppose that he expected to lie in the mausoleum of kings, where also he had buried his favourite daughter, his sister, and his venerable mother. We have no record of his expressing any wish, or giving any directions concerning his funeral, so that it scarcely admits of a doubt that the Protector was resolved that he, with his whole family, should lie among the monarchs of England; indicating thereby how completely he regarded himself as the founder of a royal dynasty.

Appendices

From
The Fall of the House of Usher
by
Edgar Allan Poe

Our books—the books which, for years, had formed no small portion of the mental existence of the invalid—were, as might be supposed, in strict keeping with this character of phantasm. We pored together over such works as the Ververt et Chartreuse of Gresset; the Belphegor of Machiavelli; the Heaven and Hell of Swedenborg; the Subterranean Voyage of Nicholas Klimm by Holberg; the Chiromancy of Robert Flud, of Jean D'Indaginé, and of De la Chambre; the Journey into the Blue Distance of Tieck; and the City of the Sun of Campanella. One favorite volume was a small octavo edition of the *Directorium Inquisitorium*, by the Dominican Eymeric de Gironne; and there were passages in Pomponius Mela, about the old African Satyrs and Œgipans, over which Usher would sit dreaming for hours. His chief delight, however, was found in the perusal of an exceedingly rare and curious book in quarto Gothic— the manual of a forgotten church—the *Vigiliæ Mortuorum secundum Chorum Ecclesiæ Maguntinæ*.

"Consider Don Quixote as an example; it is, I suppose, the finest prose romance in existence. Essentially, it expresses the eternal quest of the unknown, that longing, peculiar to man, which makes him reach out towards infinity; and he lifts up his eyes, and he strains his eyes, looking across the ocean, for certain fabled, happy islands, for Avalon that is beyond the setting of the sun. And he comes into life from the unknown world, from glorious places, and all his days he journeys through the world, spying about him, going on and ever on, expecting beyond every hill to find the holy city, seeing signs, and omens, and tokens by the way, reminded every hour of his everlasting citizenship. From the great deep to the great deep he goes..."

"The eternal moral, then, of "Don Quixote" is the strife between temporal and eternal, between the soul and the body, between things spiritual and things corporal, between ecstasy and the common life."

"It seems a mere comic incident when the knight dreaming of enchantment is knocked about, and made ridiculous; but I tell you it is the perpetual tragedy of life itself, symbolised."

—Arthur Machen
Hieroglyphics (1902)

From *Don Quixote* by Miguel de Cervantes

Chapter VI.

Of the Diverting and Important Scrutiny
Which the Curate and the Barber Made
in the Library of Our Ingenious Gentleman

He was still sleeping; so the curate asked the niece for the keys of the room where the books, the authors of all the mischief, were, and right willingly she gave them. They all went in, the housekeeper with them, and found more than a hundred volumes of big books very well bound, and some other small ones. The moment the housekeeper saw them she turned about and ran out of the room, and came back immediately with a saucer of holy water and a sprinkler, saying, "Here, your worship, señor licentiate, sprinkle this room; don't leave any magician of the many there are in these books to bewitch us in revenge for our design of banishing them from the world."

The simplicity of the housekeeper made the licentiate laugh, and he directed the barber to give him the books one by one to see what they were about, as there might be some to be found among them that did not deserve the penalty of fire.

"No," said the niece, "there is no reason for showing mercy to any of them; they have every one of them done mischief; better fling them out of the window into the court and make a pile of them and set fire to them; or else carry them into the yard, and there a bonfire can be made without the smoke giving any annoyance." The housekeeper said the same, so eager were they both for the slaughter of those innocents, but the curate would not agree to it without first reading at any rate the titles.

The first that Master Nicholas put into his hand was "*The Four Books of Amadis of Gaul*." "This seems a mysterious thing," said the curate, "for, as I have heard say, this was the first book of chivalry printed in Spain, and from this all the others derive their birth and origin; so it seems to me that we ought inexorably to condemn it to the flames as the founder of so vile a sect."

"Nay, sir," said the barber, "I too, have heard say that this is the best of all the books of this kind that have been written, and so, as something singular in its line, it ought to be pardoned."

"True," said the curate; "and for that reason let its life be spared for the present. Let us see that other which is next to it."

"It is," said the barber, "the *Sergas de Esplandian*, the lawful son of Amadis of Gaul."

"Then verily," said the curate, "the merit of the father must not be put down to the account of the son. Take it, mistress housekeeper; open the window and fling it into the yard and lay the foundation of the pile for the bonfire we are to make."

The housekeeper obeyed with great satisfaction, and the worthy "Esplandian" went flying into the yard to await with all patience the fire that was in store for him.

"Proceed," said the curate.

"This that comes next," said the barber, "is *Amadis of Greece*, and, indeed, I believe all those on this side are of the same *Amadis* lineage."

"Then to the yard with the whole of them," said the curate; "for to have the burning of Queen Pintiquiniestra, and the shepherd Darinel and his eclogues, and the bedevilled and involved discourses of his author, I would burn with them the father who begot me if he were going about in the guise of a knight-errant."

"I am of the same mind," said the barber.

"And so am I," added the niece.

"In that case," said the housekeeper, "here, into the yard with them!"

They were handed to her, and as there were many of them, she spared herself the staircase, and flung them down out of the window.

"Who is that tub there?" said the curate.

"This," said the barber, "is *Don Olivante de Laura*."

"The author of that book," said the curate, "was the same that wrote *The Garden of Flowers*, and truly there is no deciding which of the two books is the more truthful, or, to put it better, the less lying; all I can say is, send this one into the yard for a swaggering fool."

"This that follows is *Florismarte of Hircania*," said the barber.

"Señor Florismarte here?" said the curate; "then by my faith he must take up his quarters in the yard, in spite of his marvellous birth and visionary adventures, for the stiffness and dryness of his style deserve nothing else; into the yard with him and the other, mistress housekeeper."

"With all my heart, señor," said she, and executed the order with great delight.

"This," said the barber, "is *The Knight Platir*."

"An old book that," said the curate, "but I find no reason for clemency in it; send it after the others without appeal;" which was done.

Another book was opened, and they saw it was entitled, *The Knight of the Cross.*

"For the sake of the holy name this book has," said the curate, "its ignorance might be excused; but then, they say, 'behind the cross there's the devil;' to the fire with it."

Taking down another book, the barber said, "This is The *Mirror of Chivalry.*"

"I know his worship," said the curate; "that is where Señor Reinaldos of Montalvan figures with his friends and comrades, greater thieves than Cacus, and the Twelve Peers of France with the veracious historian Turpin; however, I am not for condemning them to more than perpetual banishment, because, at any rate, they have some share in the invention of the famous Matteo Boiardo, whence too the Christian poet Ludovico Ariosto wove his web, to whom, if I find him here, and speaking any language but his own, I shall show no respect whatever; but if he speaks his own tongue I will put him upon my head."

"Well, I have him in Italian," said the barber, "but I do not understand him."

"Nor would it be well that you should understand him," said the curate, "and on that score we might have excused the Captain if he had not brought him into Spain and turned him into Castilian. He robbed him of a great deal of his natural force, and so do all those who try to turn books written in verse into another language, for, with all the pains they take and all the cleverness they show, they never can reach the level of the originals as they were first produced. In short, I say that this book, and all that may be found treating of those French affairs, should be thrown into or deposited in some dry well, until after more consideration it is settled what is to be done with them; excepting always one *Bernardo del Carpio* that is going about, and another called *Roncesvalles*; for these, if they come into my hands, shall pass at once into those of the housekeeper, and from hers into the fire without any reprieve."

To all this the barber gave his assent, and looked upon it as right and proper, being persuaded that the curate was so staunch to the Faith and loyal to the Truth that he would not for the world say anything opposed to them. Opening another book he saw it was *Palmerin de Oliva*, and beside it was another called *Palmerin of England*, seeing which the licentiate said, "Let the Olive be made firewood of at once and burned until no ashes even are left; and let that Palm of England be kept and preserved as a thing that stands alone, and let such another case be made for it as that which Alexander found among the spoils of Darius and set aside for the safe keeping of the works of the poet Homer. This book, gossip, is of authority for two reasons, first because it is very good, and secondly because it is said to have been written by a wise and witty king of Portugal. All the adventures at the Castle of Miraguarda are excellent and of admirable contrivance, and the language is polished and clear, studying and observing the style befitting the speaker with propriety and judgment. So then, provided it seems good to you, Master Nicholas, I say let this and *Amadis of Gaul* be remitted the penalty of fire, and as for all the rest, let them perish without further question or query."

"Nay, gossip," said the barber, "for this that I have here is the famous *Don Belianis*."

"Well," said the curate, "that and the second, third, and fourth parts all stand in need of a little rhubarb to purge their excess of bile, and they must be cleared of all that stuff about the Castle of Fame and other greater affectations, to which end let them be allowed the over-seas term, and, according as they mend, so shall mercy or justice be meted out to them; and in the mean time, gossip, do you keep them in your house and let no one read them."

"With all my heart," said the barber; and not caring to tire himself with reading more books of chivalry, he told the housekeeper to take all the big ones and throw them into the yard. It was not said to one dull or deaf, but to one who enjoyed burning them more than weaving the broadest and finest web that could be; and seizing about eight at a time, she flung them out of the window.

In carrying so many together she let one fall at the feet of the barber, who took it up, curious to know whose it was, and found it said, *History of the Famous Knight, Tirante el Blanco*."

"God bless me!" said the curate with a shout, "*Tirante el Blanco* here! Hand it over, gossip, for in it I reckon I have found a treasury of enjoyment and a mine of recreation. Here is Don Kyrieleison of Montalvan, a valiant knight, and his brother Thomas of Montalvan, and the knight Fonseca, with the battle the bold Tirante fought with the mastiff, and the witticisms of the damsel Placerdemivida, and the loves and wiles of the widow Reposada, and the empress in love with the squire Hipolito—in truth, gossip, by right of its style it is the best book in the world. Here knights eat and sleep, and die in their beds, and make their wills before dying, and a great deal more of which there is nothing in all the other books. Nevertheless, I say he who wrote it, for deliberately composing such fooleries, deserves to be sent to the galleys for life. Take it home with you and read it, and you will see that what I have said is true."

"As you will," said the barber; "but what are we to do with these little books that are left?"

"These must be, not chivalry, but poetry," said the curate; and opening one he saw it was the *Diana* of Jorge de Montemayor, and, supposing all the others to be of the same sort, "these," he said, "do not deserve to be burned like the others, for they neither do nor can do the mischief the books of chivalry have done, being books of entertainment that can hurt no one."

"Ah, señor!" said the niece, "your worship had better order these to be burned as well as the others; for it would be no wonder if, after being cured of his chivalry disorder, my uncle, by reading these, took a fancy to turn shepherd and range the woods and fields singing and piping; or, what would be still worse, to turn poet, which they say is an incurable and infectious malady."

"The damsel is right," said the curate, "and it will be well to put this stumbling-block and temptation out of our friend's way. To begin, then, with the *Diana* of Montemayor. I am of opinion it should not be burned, but that it should be cleared of all that about the sage Felicia and the magic water, and of almost all the longer pieces of verse: let it keep, and welcome, its prose and the honour of being the first of books of the kind."

"This that comes next," said the barber, "is the *Diana*, entitled the 'Second Part, by the Salamancan,' and this other has the same title, and its author is Gil Polo."

"As for that of the Salamancan," replied the curate, "let it go to swell the number of the condemned in the yard, and let Gil Polo's be preserved as if it came from Apollo himself: but get on, gossip, and make haste, for it is growing late."

"This book," said the barber, opening another, "is *The Ten Books of the Fortune of Love*, written by Antonio de Lofraso, a Sardinian poet."

"By the orders I have received," said the curate, "since Apollo has been Apollo, and the Muses have been Muses, and poets have been poets, so droll and absurd a book as this has never been written, and in its way it is the best and the most singular of all of this species that have as yet appeared, and he who has not read it may be sure he has never read what is delightful. Give it here, gossip, for I make more account of having found it than if they had given me a cassock of Florence stuff."

He put it aside with extreme satisfaction, and the barber went on, "These that come next are *The Shepherd of Iberia, Nymphs of Henares,* and *The Enlightenment of Jealousy.*"

"Then all we have to do," said the curate, "is to hand them over to the secular arm of the housekeeper, and ask me not why, or we shall never have done."

"This next is the *Pastor de Fílida.*"

"No Pastor that," said the curate, "but a highly polished courtier; let it be preserved as a precious jewel."

"This large one here," said the barber, "is called *The Treasury of Various Poems.*"

"If there were not so many of them," said the curate, "they would be more relished: this book must be weeded and cleansed of certain vulgarities which it has with its excellences; let it be preserved because the author is a friend of mine, and out of respect for other more heroic and loftier works that he has written."

"This," continued the barber, "is *The Cancionero* of Lopez de Maldonado."

"The author of that book, too," said the curate, "is a great friend of mine, and his verses from his own mouth are the admiration of all who hear them, for such is the sweetness of his voice that he enchants when he chants them: it gives rather too much of its eclogues, but what is good was never yet plentiful: let it be kept with those that have been set apart. But what book is that next it?"

"The *Galatea* of Miguel de Cervantes," said the barber.

"That Cervantes has been for many years a great friend of mine, and to my knowledge he has had more experience in reverses than in verses. His book has some good invention in it, it presents us with something but brings nothing to a conclusion: we must wait for the Second Part it promises: perhaps with amendment it may succeed in winning the full measure of grace that is now denied it; and in the mean time do you, señor gossip, keep it shut up in your own quarters."

"Very good," said the barber; "and here come three together, *The Araucana* of Don Alonso de Ercilla, *The Austriada* of Juan Rufo, Justice of Cordova, and *The Montserrate* of Christobal de Virués, the Valencian poet."

"These three books," said the curate, "are the best that have been written in Castilian in heroic verse, and they may compare with the most famous of Italy; let them be preserved as the richest treasures of poetry that Spain possesses."

The curate was tired and would not look into any more books, and so he decided that, "contents uncertified," all the rest should be burned; but just then the barber held open one, called *The Tears of Angelica*.

"I should have shed tears myself," said the curate when he heard the title, "had I ordered that book to be burned, for its author was one of the famous poets of the world, not to say of Spain, and was very happy in the translation of some of Ovid's fables."

Bibliography of Books Reviewed

"Visitation of the Monasteries in the Reign of Henry the Eighth." is likely referring to *The Letters and Papers of Henry VIII., Volume X.* Edited by James Gairdner (London; Her Majesty's Stationery Office, 1887).

The Vision of William concerning Piers the Plowman; together with Richard the Redeless. Edited by Professor Skeat. Two vols. (Oxford; Clarendon Press, 1886).

The Blood Covenant by H. Clay Trumbull, D.D. (Redway, 1887).

Christopher Marlowe. Edited by Havelock Ellis. Unexpurgated Edition. (Vizetelly & Co., 1887).

Syrian Stone-Lore by Claude Regnier Conder, R.E. (Bentley & Son, 1887).

Phantasms of the Living by Edmund Gurney, M.A., Frederick W. H. Myers, M.A., and Frank Podmore, M.A. Two vols. (Trübner & Co., 1886).

The Influence of Italian upon English Literature by J. Ross Murray, B.A. (Cambridge; Deighton, Bell & Co., 1886).

The Trade Signs of Essex by Miller Christy (Griffith, Farran, & Co., 1887).

La Vie Privée d'autrefois : Arts et Métiers, Modes, Mœurs, Usages des Parisiens du xiie au xviiie Siècle par Alfred Franklin. 12mo. Vols, i., ii. (Paris; Plon, 1887).

The Marriage of Cupid and Psyche. Done into English by William Adlington, with a Discourse on the Fable by Andrew Lang. (London; David Nutt, 1887).

Palæolithic Man in N.W. Middlesex by John Allen Brown. (London; MacMillan, 1887).

Sketches of Life in Japan by Major Henry Knollys. (Chapman & Hall, 1887).

The First Nine Years of the Bank of England by J. E. Thorold Rogers. (The Clarendon Press, 1887).

The Brunswick Accession by Percy M. Thornton. (William Ridgway, 1887).

History of the Bassandyne Bible . . . with Notices of the Early Printers of Edinburgh by William T. Dobson. (Edinburgh; Blackwood & Sons, 1887).

A Proposal for putting Reform to the Vote by the Hermit of Marlow (P. B. Shelley). (The Shelley Society, 1887).

The Purpose of the Ages by Jeanie Morison. (Macmillan & Co., 1887).

Hungary in Ancient, Mediæval, and Modern Times by Arminius Vambéry. (T. Fisher Unwin, 1887).

The Sieges of Pontefract Castle, 1644—1648. Edited by Richard Holmes. (Pontefract; Richard Holmes, 1887).

Memoir of the Family of M'Combie by W. M'Combie Smith. (Edinburgh; Blackwood & Sons, 1887).

Histoire de la Poésie Liturgique au Moyen Age. Les Tropes par Léon Gautier, Professeur à l'Ecole des Chartes. 8vo., vol. i. (Paris; Victor Palmé et Al. Picard, 1886).

Shropshire Folk- Lore: A Sheaf of Gleanings. Edited by Charlotte Sophia Burne, from the Collections of Georgina F. Jackson. Part III. (Trübner & Co, 1886).

Herefordshire Words and Phrases by Francis T. Havergal, M.A. (Walsall; W. H. Robinson, 1887).

Chronicles of An Old Inn; or, A Few Words about Gray's Inn by Andrée Hope. (Chapman & Hall, 1887).

The Parish Registers of Kirkburton, co. York. Edited by Frances Anne Collins. Vol. i. (Exeter; W. Pollard & Co., 1887).

Epitaphs; or, Churchyard Gleanings, collected by Old Mortality. (Ranken & Co., 1887).

The Saracens from the Earliest Times to the Fall of Bagdad by Arthur Gilman. (T. Fisher Unwin, 1887).

The Gnostics and their Remains, Ancient and Mediæval by C. W. King. (David Nutt, 1887).

ARTHUR MACHEN
Selected Works

FICTION

Novels

The Three Impostors (1895)

Hill of Dreams (1907)

The Terror (1917)

The Secret Glory (1922)

The Green Round (1933)

Novellas

The Great God Pan (1894) Includes *The Inmost Light.*

House of Souls (1906) Collection which includes *A Fragment of Life* and *The White People.*

The Great Return (1915)

Short Story Collections

*The Angel of Mons: The Bowmen
and Other Legends of the War* (1915)

Ornaments in Jade (1924)

The Shining Pyramid (1925)

The Cosy Room (1936)

The Children of the Pool (1936)

Other Fiction

Eleusinia (1881) Poetry.

The Anatomy of Tobacco (1884)

The Chronicle of Clemendy (1888)

NONFICTION

Memoirs

Far Off Things (1922)

Things Near and Far (1923)

The London Adventure (1924)

Essays

Strange Roads (1923)

Dog and Duck (1924)

Dreads and Drolls (1926)

Notes and Queries (1926)

Tom O'Bedlam and His Song (1930)

Bridles and Spurs (1951)

Mist and Mystery (2022)

Miscellaneous Nonfiction

Hieroglyphics (1902) Literary criticism.

The House of the Hidden Light (1904) With A. E. Waite.

Dr. Stiggins, His Views and Principles (1906) Religious criticism.

War and the Christian Faith (1918) Christian apologetics.

Precious Balms (1926) Literary criticism.

The Canning Wonder (1925) Historical criticism.

A Reader of Curious Books (2020) Literary and antiquarian criticism.

Translations

The Heptameron (1886)

The Way to Attain (1889)

The Memoirs of Casanova (1894)

Remarks Upon Hermodactylus (1933)

References

Danielson, Henry. *Arthur Machen, A Bibliography* (London; Henry Danielson, 1923).

Goldstone, Adrian & Sweester, Wesley D. *Bibliography of Arthur Machen* (University of Texas Press, 1965).

Machen, Arthur.
—*The Three Impostors* (London; Grant Richards, 1895).
—*Hieroglyphics* (London; Grant Richards, 1902).
—*The House of Souls* (London; Grant Richards, 1906).
—*The Secret Glory* (London; Martin Secker, 1922).
—*Far Off Things* (London; Martin Secker, 1922).
—*Things Near and Far* (London; Martin Secker, 1923).
—*Dog and Duck: A London Calendar Et Cætera* (New York; Alfred A. Knopf, 1924).
—*The London Adventure* (London; Martin Secker, 1924).
—*The Green Round* (London; Ernest Benn Limited, 1933).
—*The Cosy Room* (London; Rich & Cowan, Ltd, 1936).

Reynolds, Aiden & Charlton, William. *Arthur Machen* (London; The Richards Press, 1963).

Sweester, Wesley D. *Arthur Machen* (New York; Twayne, 1964).

Books by Arthur Machen

Available from Darkly Bright Press

The Great Return, Annotated Edition: Includes the classic novella, *The Sangraal, Parts I-III*, new essays and appreciations.

A Reader of Curious Books: A collection of rare material previously unavailable since its original 1887 publication in the *Walford's Antiquarian Magazine*.

Mist and Mystery: Recovered stories and essays by Arthur Machen from the pages of *T. P.'s Weekly*.

Dreamt in Fire—The Expanded Second Edition: An original collection of Machen's fiction and essays which provides a comprehensive survey of his work.

Out of Print

A Secret Language: A miniature manifesto by Machen on his approach to literature and Christian mysticism. Annotated.

Levavi Oculos: The brilliant short story which highlights an application of Machen's literary theory. Annotated.

Hardcover Editions are available. To place an order, please visit *darklybrightpress.com* and read rare Arthur Machen material posted every week.

DRINKING HEALTHS IN SAXON TIMES.